Praise for *And the War Is Over:*

"[A] poignant first novel . . . All the ingredients for an updated *Bridge on the River Kwai* are present—the cruel, inscrutable but vaguely honorable Japanese commanders, the abused European prisoners of war, the exotic and perilous tropics, the ironies and the manhood-testing opportunities inherent in popular literature about World War II. But Ismail Marahimin is not interested in the Europeans' view of the war. What is remarkable about *And the War Is Over* is that we finally get the familiar war from an unfamiliar, non-combatant, Asian point of view. . . . The Sumatran jungle, with its tigers, its fish, its mosquitoes, its deep green brush and its swamps."
　　—Bharati Mukherjee, *The Washington Post Book World*

"*And the War Is Over* . . . has the dramatic intensity of a kick in the guts. . . . Marahimin writes simply and honesty from the omniscient-author perspective, shifting at will from character to character. Though his sympathies must surely lie with the Indonesians, Marahimin somehow manages to assign equal legitimacy to the thoughts and values of the Dutch and Japanese. His mastery of the universe he's created is flawless. The novel's denouement is shocking, for it underscores the fundamental social principle that the clash of cultures, especially in wartime, wreaks its greatest toll on the innocent. It underscores a corollary to that proposition, too, that at such times innocence is a fateful—and fatal—luxury."
　　—Denny Clements, *The Philadelphia Inquirer*

"The book's images are rich and unusual . . . the characters foreign and intriguing. . . . The author's wish to show how all people, no matter what their origins, are but pawns on a larger chessboard. *And the War Is Over* is a fascinating glimpse at people gasping for air in another corner of the world where war sounds painfully familiar."
　　—*San Francisco Chronicle Book Review*

"*And the War Is Over* suggests a deceptively clear drop of tropical river water seen under a relentless fictional microscope. A small detachment of Japanese soldiers, the Dutch prisoners of war they guard, and the Indonesians who are pressed into service or who look on from the village all intertwine in Marahimin's superficially simple narrative, shifting, mingling, writing, dying. . . . *And the War Is Over,* Marahimin's first novel, humanizes dehumanization in yet another parable of lives shattered forever by war. His people, achingly real, learn nothing from their uncomprehending roles in a conflict they will never understand, surviving—if they do—as broken pieces of the men and women they used to be. . . . Marahimin demonstrates that the history man makes is only an empty gesture, and the tradition his villagers live is the only life that can survive—another illustration from Third World fiction that there may be more than one definition for civilization." —Mitzi Brunsdale, *Houston Post*

"This deep and complex novel by Indonesian writer Ismail Marahimin depicts the strained final weeks of World War II in a small Sumatran village. . . . The author is able to handle several diverse plots deftly, but this book's greatest strength is its portrayal of decent, average people under pressure. It points up what the deepest corners of our human hearts will ultimately have us do. . . . The author is searching for redemption for all humans as he points up what war really means." —Abigail F. Davis, *Rocky Mountain News*

"Cultures may clash, but the humanity of all is evident in this thoughtful novel that shows us the horror of war from a new perspective." —L. M. Lewis, *Library Journal*

And the War Is Over

THE PEGASUS PRIZE FOR LITERATURE

AND THE WAR IS OVER

A Novel by ISMAIL MARAHIMIN

Translated by John H. McGlynn

GROVE PRESS
New York

This Grove Press edition is published by arrangement with Louisiana State University Press.

Published simultaneously in Canada
Printed in the United States of America

FIRST GROVE PRESS EDITION

Library of Congress Cataloging-in-Publication Data

Marahimin, Ismail, 1934–
    [Dan perang pun usai. English]
    And the war is over : a novel / by Ismail Marahimin ; translated by John H. McGlynn.
        p. cm.
    Translation of: Dan perang pun usai.
    ISBN 0-8021-3922-1
    1. World War, 1939–1945—Indonesia—Fiction. 2. Indonesia—History—Japanese occupation, 1942–1945—Fiction. I. Title.

PL5089.M356 D313 2002
899'.22133—dc21   2002021379

Grove Press
841 Broadway
New York, NY 10003

02 03 04 05   10 9 8 7 6 5 4 3 2 1

Contents

Publisher's Note

The Pegasus Prize for Literature, created by Mobil Corporation in 1977 and published by Louisiana State University Press since 1980, recognizes distinguished works of fiction from countries whose literature merits wider exposure in the rest of the world. *And the War Is Over,* by Ismail Marahimin, was awarded the Pegasus Prize in Indonesia in October 1984, after a committee of distinguished scholars and editors selected it from among the best Indonesian novels written in the past decade. Completed in 1977, *And the War Is Over* is Mr. Marahimin's first novel.

Chairman of the Pegasus Prize selection committee was Subagyo Sastrowardoyo, a director of the state-run publishing company, Balai Pustaka. Other members of the jury were H. B. Jassin, the first man to do a verse translation of the Koran into Indonesian; Umar Kayam, author and director of the Cultural Studies Center, University of Gajah Mada, Yogyakarta; and Boen Umarjati and Sapardi Djoko Damano, both lecturers at the University of Indonesia.

The novel is set in a village in Sumatra where Dutch prisoners of war and forced workers from Java have been incarcerated by the Japanese army during World War II. Unaware that the war is about to end, the internees plan an escape into the jungles of Sumatra. The tragic irony of their mistimed escape triggers the drama in this brief, tensely drawn novel about three cultures, each alien to the others.

The translator, John McGlynn, is a resident of Jakarta. His previous translations include *A Taste of Betel and Lime,* an anthology of poetry by Indonesian women; *Reflections on Rebellion: Stories on Indonesian Upheavals of 1948 and 1965;* and *Shackles,* a prerevolution Indonesian novel. He also subtitles Indonesian films.

Grove/Atlantic, Inc., joins Louisiana State University Press in expressing appreciation to Mobil Corporation, which established the Pegasus Prize for Literature, and provides for the translation into English of the works the award honors. As publisher of this paperback edition, Grove/Atlantic also wishes to express gratitude to Louisiana State University Press, which has published all but the first of the Pegasus Prize winners in hardcover, for making this work available in English for the first time and for allowing us to join it in this endeavor.

And the War Is Over

ONE

Vader Jacob, Vader Jacob,
Slaapt hij nog? Slaapt hij nog?
Hoor de klokken luiden, hoor de klokken luiden,
Bim, bam, bom; bim, bam, bom.

Are you sleeping, are you sleeping,
Brother John, Brother John?
Morning bells are ringing, morning bells are ringing,
Ding, dong, ding; ding, dong, ding.

The Dutch internees were working too hard. Carefully and silently, seldom making a mistake, they rarely needed a reminder or an order from the Japanese soldier supervising them. They seemed to have a sixth sense that told them where to heap the earth they shouldered and how to tamp it with their bare feet to strengthen the western side of the embankment in which they had already driven rows of stakes. Back to the eastern side, down the embankment, and six or seven meters beyond, they picked up their full, but not too full, baskets of earth. The twelve men assigned to fill the baskets carried out their task with practiced ease; those whose job it was to carry the baskets never had to wait for one to be filled. And never once did the guard have to urge on the Dutch with "Come on, get those baskets filled!"

Sergeant Kiguchi pondered the scene before him. What was in the air? he wondered. The memory of what had happened a month before, early in the third week after their

1

move to this site on the southern bank of the Kampar Kanan River, was still fresh. There had been an open altercation between Wimpie, a boxer and a sergeant in the Royal Dutch Army, and Dem, a sergeant in the Royal Dutch Navy who had been a member of the Dutch swimming team at the Berlin Olympiad in 1936. Two days later Dem was killed in an accident, his skull crushed by a rail that was being unloaded from the train. An accident!

Yesterday one of the soldiers had told Kiguchi about the atmosphere at the work site, and today he had come to observe the scene for himself. It was true. The Dutch were trying their best not to attract attention but, precisely because of their silence and their serious demeanor, the opposite was the case. He knew immediately that they were trying to keep something secret. Their faces showed tension and hope for revenge. They were biding their time.

Kiguchi was experienced in handling such matters. Supposing that he were the commander and not Lieutenant Ose he would act immediately. In the past his swiftness of manner had caused the death of six or seven detainees. A fair number of Dutch internees, *romusha*, and civilians as well had suffered broken bones or other physical damage at his hands. His style had done little to raise him in rank but he didn't mind. An enemy was an enemy and should be treated as such, even if he had surrendered. If the enemy won Kiguchi would be treated in the same manner. As for the *romusha*, well they were a colonized class of people, little better than slaves.

Lieutenant Ose, the present commander, was a different sort of person. In fact, the commander was the oddest Japanese military officer Kiguchi had ever come across. He was soft-spoken, friendly, patient, and mindful of detail. Covertly, Kiguchi respected the man but he himself preferred being a man of action. After all, the Dai Nippon Army had been created to act, hadn't it?

The nine soldiers in the barracks seemed to share Kiguchi's opinions. In particular, they disagreed with the manner in which Ose had settled the incident with Dem. The

2

affair had drawn them even closer to one another and appeared to be the reason why they had reported to Kiguchi on the change in behavior of the Dutch internees and not to Lieutenant Ose.

Kiguchi wondered what it was the Dutch prisoners here in the village of Taratakbuluh were lacking. In Pakanbaru they had been forced to work all day and had been constantly beaten and tortured. There had never been enough food for them and they had been compelled to sleep squashed together in barracks that were far too small. Compared with that, their life here was heaven.

On the day of their arrival in Taratakbuluh, the new sense of freedom this place offered was readily apparent: the Dutch shouted like little children and collected fruit from rubber trees to roast and eat. On the second day at the camp, they clambered about the numerous cashew trees that skirted the bed of reeds at the river's edge. Not satisfied with eating only the apples, they roasted and ate the outer nuts as well. During the three days that followed, the internees were kept busy cutting down reeds around the place where they bathed and setting out the fish traps they had made from the left-over pieces of bamboo that lay in profusion around the barracks. Inside the barracks they kept a fire burning to roast the fish and yams that Freddie, the cook, purchased at the market. Even though the daily budget was the same as it had been in Pakanbaru, goods in this village were much cheaper.

What was the consequence of this freedom and fun? They had fought and now one of them was dead. Kiguchi was sure that Dem had been murdered and that Wimpie was his killer but Lieutenant Ose did nothing about it. What could he say? Lieutenant Ose was the commander, and the commander was the representative of *Tennō Heika*, the emperor, incarnation and representative of the gods.

When the bell sounded twice, signaling that it was two o'clock Tokyo time or eleven thirty local time, the detainees were allowed a half hour rest. Freddie came out with food for the other prisoners, unassisted by Kliwon, the *romusha* who had been assigned to help him. He carried a basket of bowls in his left hand and in his right an oil tin that had been converted into a cooking pot. The men's entire ration of food for the noonday meal was in that kerosene tin: a little rice, cassava, noodles made from sago flour, a little animal fat, a few vegetables, and some spices all cooked together into a porridge.

Today, unlike other days, none of the Dutch pushed or shouted or demanded a larger portion of food. Wimpie made an obvious attempt to liven up the atmosphere.

"What's on the menu for today, Auntie?" he asked one of the men in Dutch.

The man he addressed said nothing. While Kiguchi couldn't understand Dutch he could sense that Wimpie was making fun of the man. Only a few of the men, Wimpie's friends, appeared to respond.

"Hey, Auntie!" Wimpie shouted again, "How many times have I told you I don't like my steak well done? I like it raw, completely raw!"

Kiguchi could detect two groups, the one headed by Wimpie and the other by van Roscott. Van Roscott was an assistant chaplain and even though he carried the rank of lieutenant in the Royal Dutch Army he was still called "Pastor" by the other detainees. There appeared to be a third group as well, this one in the middle with Freddie as its leader. Regardless of the number, Wimpie was definitely the reason behind the formation and makeup of the groups.

Kiguchi began to think of *sumo* or *jujitsu* moves that he could use to fell Wimpie. That gorilla would not be safe. One blow would be sufficient to paralyze or possibly kill the man. He would have no chance at all.

And Kliwon? Where had that insolent *romusha* gone off to now? he wondered. It was beyond Kiguchi why Kliwon had been brought along with this group of men. His name had not been on the original list of transfers but suddenly, out of the blue, he was there with them on the train. And here he had no real job to do except stick out his hand to receive a daily allowance that was twice as large as the one

4

given to the Dutch internees. Lieutenant Ose didn't do anything about him either. Kliwon should be run out of camp, the usual disposition of *romusha* who had outlived their usefulness.

Seven thirty Tokyo time. The Dutch stopped working. Their shovels and baskets were collected and counted. The men formed rows; it was their turn to be counted. Thirty plus Freddie, who was now fixing the evening meal. All accounted for.

Keeping in a neat line, the Dutch walked toward the barracks located not too far to the west of the work site. Pastor had been designated by the Japanese authorities as leader of the group and he walked out front and somewhat to the right of the line. Wimpie and his men kept to the back. In the center of the line, with more men than either the front or back group, was the middle group. All the men were young and in terms of physical health had been among the best from the thousands of detainees who were scattered in camps throughout the Riau area at the time they were sent here. Now most of them were thin and their shaven heads, thick mustaches, unkempt beards, and ragged uniforms gave them a pitiful and disgusting appearance. Nonetheless, in their eyes there shone a light, one unlike the light in the eyes of the thousands of other people living in the region and even more unlike the light in the eyes of the thousands of men who had died. In their eyes shone the light of revenge.

Wimpie attempted to inject some cheer into the atmosphere.

"Hey, we're not dead yet," he shouted, "let's sing something like we usually do."

Wimpie and the men in his group began to sing. The other two groups offered no refrain. Soon the short song was over and not begun again.

"Christ, this is like a funeral procession," Wimpie muttered accusingly.

The evening roll call was convened at eight o'clock sharp, Tokyo time. Local time, it was only 5:30 P.M. The ten Japa-

5

nese soldiers and the thirty-one Dutch detainees lined up in pairs to form two wide rows. The men faced eastward, their backs to the three woven bamboo buildings that formed the small camp. One of the buildings was Lieutenant Ose's lodgings. Another, the security post, doubled as the soldiers' barracks. Then there was the barracks for the internees. Standing on a makeshift dais in front of the men, Lieutenant Ose first listened to Sergeant Kiguchi's report in Japanese and then to Pastor's report in Indonesian. Nothing had happened that warranted his special attention. Everything was going smoothly. The *Hinomaru*, the Rising Sun, was lowered from its place atop the bamboo flagpole. The men were dismissed.

This evening the detainees didn't bolt off toward the dinner table they had made by nailing three wooden planks across the stumps of two rubber trees situated between their barracks and the security post. They walked at a leisurely pace. Freddie went immediately into action and from his kerosene tin began to ladle porridge into the bowls already sitting on top of the table. The men ate in groups and spoke in half-whispered voices.

After their meal the men went down to the river to bathe and to check their fish traps which they filled with new bait as they balanced themselves in a squatting position atop a board they had placed there for that purpose.

"We internees are an elite group of men," Wimpie often said on these nightly trips. "We don't eat shit here. The fish eat our shit and then we eat the fish."

Usually Wimpie and his jokes excited some kind of reaction, but this evening even he was silent. No one shouted about his catch of fish or displayed what he had found in his trap. The men took their time tending to their bodily needs and then returned to the barracks to roast fish or cashew nuts on the fire that Freddie prepared each evening between the two long *balai*. Beside the makeshift hearth was a small clay bowl of salt. It was Tuesday, mid August in the year 2605 *Showa* of the Japanese calendrical system or A.D. 1945, and the men's supply of cassava was gone. Those who hadn't any fish or cashews to roast sat quietly watching their friends enjoy their extra meal.

❁

It is difficult if not impossible to fathom the ins and outs of human life. Who determines where a person is born, where he will raise his children, where he will be buried? While one person might be born at the North Pole, spend his life on the equator, and die at the South Pole another person might never leave the village in which he was born. There seems to be a kind of master train schedule regulating the course of human life, determining where a person must be and what time he must be there to meet those who are destined to escort him onward to happiness, disaster, or perhaps only to the memory of a chance and fleeting encounter.

First Lieutenant Gentaro Ose was born in Osaka, a city which long before the eruption of the Pacific War was already an industrial giant. Ose's father had nothing to do with that, however. He was only a postman, always friendly and polite, always a humble smile on his face but not a man with people working beneath him and not a man born to climb the social ladder. Compared with his father, Lieutenant Ose was a man of significant advantage. He was a commander with authority over forty-two people: ten Japanese soldiers, thirty-one Dutch internees, and one *romusha*, Kliwon, the cook's helper. In one respect, however, Lieutenant Ose and his father were similar. Promotion had never come easily to the younger Ose. Ose had joined the military with the rank of second lieutenant and since that time had been promoted only once—when a mass promotion was handed out after the success of the Long March down the coast of Southeast Asia and the capture of Singapore, which was subsequently renamed Shonanto. That had been in 2602 *Showa* or 1942 and now three years later he was still a first lieutenant. Meanwhile, many of his classmates had risen to the rank of captain or even major. Of course, many others now lay buried in unknown lands and in unknown seas.

It is not usually the lower social strata of a culture who maintain the traditions that outsiders view as characteristics specific to that culture. Or if they do, it is in a watered-down form which a more orthodox representative of that tradition would find upsetting if not shameful. It is not surprising therefore that Ose was very uncomfortable and caused numerous sympathetic looks the first time he shared tea at the home of Ando, the Shinto priest. He was there because Yoshie, the priest's daughter, was the girl-friend of his friend Shinji. The ceremony that day both embarrassed and pleased him, the latter because it gave him the impetus to delve further into the mysteries of this noble tradition. Whenever Shinji visited Priest Ando's home Ose went along. At first he went to study the tea ceremony, but later to see Michiko, the priest's other daughter who was a year and a half older than Yoshie.

Ose became entranced by the tea ceremony and he carried it out with a fanaticism that had more than once made him the butt of jokes among the other Japanese officers and soldiers stationed in southern Sumatra. At every available opportunity he would put on his kimono, make himself a pot of tea, and then sip the tea slowly and carefully from the small bowl that he carried with him wherever he went. A slight change had taken place in his regimen after he was assigned to be commander of the squad sent to re-strengthen the embankment of the wooden bridge that spanned the Kampar Kanan River. His friend Shinji, who was now a major and by coincidence also stationed in Pa-kanbaru, presented him with a native woman to attend to his needs. That was Satiyah. Within a few days after her ar-rival Ose had succeeded in training her to serve his tea in a reasonably skilled fashion.

After roll call on that mid-August evening in 2605 Ose hastened back to his hut, located about ten meters from the security post in the opposite direction from the inter-nees' barracks. Unlike the other two woven bamboo build-ings, his hut had a wooden floor that was raised about one meter from the ground and was made by nailing planks to beams that were fixed to living rubber trees. All three buildings in the compound used living rubber trees as corner supports. In fact, their branches hadn't even been cut off and when the wind blew, the buildings would sway, making rents in the tar paper roofs.

After bathing, Ose put on his kimono and sat before the small table that had been specially built for his eating and tea-drinking needs. Satiyah served his meal. She poured his tea and sat opposite him, legs beneath her in Japanese style. Occasionally Ose would glance at the woman's face. She was pretty. Young too, probably no more than twenty-five years old, and her full breasts and dusky-colored skin made her a woman of no minor attraction. Ose and Satiyah had been together for more than a month now but never once had he tried to force himself on her. Though Major Shinji had been able to overpower her, that had been for a single time only and the incident had caused an unexpected and inordinate amount of commotion. Shinji's experience together with the fear he could see on the woman's face allayed Ose's desires. Besides, he had a great deal more than sex to think about now. Of late the effect that the Greater East Asian War was having on Japan had begun to show. The last letter he received from home had been written in January, eight months earlier. Since that time the Allied bombings had continued and increased in intensity. Were his mother and father still living? How were his two children faring with their grandfather?

Headquarters in Pakanbaru had informed him numerous times throughout the day that an important piece of news was to be conveyed to all Japanese commanders in the region that night. Was it to be news of Japan's defeat? Of peace? Or the beginning of a new phase in the war, the beginning of *jibaku*, a war that would continue until the last drop of Japanese blood had been shed? The uncertainty tore him apart. Ever since childhood he had been afraid of uncertainty. Before going to bed at night, he had always checked behind the curtain that separated the area in which he slept from the area where his parents slept to see

9

if anything was there. There never was, but he looked behind the wardrobe, the vase, and the plants as well just to make sure that nothing would disturb his sleep.

The Allies had destroyed Osaka with their bombing raids some time ago. This much he knew from the military communiqués he received regularly. Was the city's postal system still operating? Was his old and now stooped father still pushing his bicycle with its basket of letters from one house to the next? No, he couldn't be dead. Ose was sure of that. An old man who bowed humbly and smiled politely at everyone he met on his daily journey—what American bullet would dare approach, much less hurt him? But what was happening to the motherland and to the struggle the Greater East Asian War represented? What had happened to Tokyo and to *Tennō Heika*? What kind of secret bomb had the United States dropped on Hiroshima and Nagasaki the week before?

With a million questions in his mind, Ose rose and walked to the corner of the room that was separated by a cloth screen. Slowly he took off his kimono and put on official dress. Every time that Ose put on the clothes that Satiyah washed for him or took out a clean shirt to wear from the locked chest in the corner of the room his fingers sought the feel of a cloth-wrapped bundle. At one time he had done this to assure himself that the bundle was still in its proper place; now he did it out of habit. Once when his fingers touched the bundle his heart would beat faster with the hope of a better life for his family after the war was over. Now it seemed there was nothing to hope for and the bundle, filled with the jewelry that Shinji had given him, excited no response at all. Ose no longer bothered to open it or take the time to admire its contents.

Ose walked slowly to the door.

"Satiyah-san," he called, "put the food on the table. Then you may go to bed." Ose spoke in Indonesian and with a respectful tone of voice. He was always respectful, even toward Satiyah, but try as he might he had yet to master the *l* sound and would find himself voicing a rolled *r*.

Ose stepped down from his hut and walked toward the security post. The soldiers on night watch had already set up small torches around the detainees' barracks. There were about twenty of these torches, which were made from finger-size pieces of rubber wrapped in dried banana leaves. The torches were changed every three hours and at night the area was alive with the flickering of light as the torches rocked in the wind. Rubber torches represented the only abundant source of lighting in the area and were used not only around the detainees' barracks on the southern side of the Kampar Kanan River but in the yards of homes in Taratakbuluh, the village located on the northern side of the river. Anyone who could afford to preferred to use palm oil candles and there were a few of these in Ose's hut, in the security post, and a couple in the prisoners' barracks.

In addition to the three soldiers on night watch, Ose found Sergeant Kiguchi in the security post as well. The sergeant led the men in saluting Lieutenant Ose. The three guards then left the post and went out to the grounds where they sat on rubber tree stumps. Ose sat down on the bench they had vacated beside Sergeant Kiguchi, who appeared to be in serious thought.

"*Konban-wa*, Kiguchi," Ose greeted.

The greeting startled Kiguchi. "*Hai!* Good evening, Ose-san," he returned while bowing his head in Ose's direction.

"Is something on your mind?" Ose inquired.

The sergeant hesitated. He didn't know whether to speak with Ose about the problem that was bothering him. But Ose was his commander and the man's humble nature sapped him of the strength to lie.

"I sense tension among the detainees," Kiguchi said listlessly.

"Like before, at the time of the incident with Dem?"

"Yes, but even more so."

"For the time being, don't do anything at all," Ose advised after thinking silently for a moment. "Keep your eyes peeled. If they start fighting, separate them. If necessary, rotate their work assignments."

11

If tension among the Dutch was on the rise, what did this mean? Ose wondered. Who was going to get killed this time? Van Roscott was clearly not Wimpie's match. Freddie wasn't either. Or were the others planning to kill Wimpie?

Or was it something else altogether? A plan to escape? That would be crazy. Where could they run? Across the river was the village but the villagers weren't likely to help the Dutch detainees. If they tried to escape by river they would end up as bait for crocodiles. To the south, behind the barracks, was virgin jungle, untouched by man and alive with wild animals.

Ose hoped that nothing would happen. This was the first and probably the last time that he would ever serve as a commander. He wanted everything to go smoothly. He hoped not to have to use force and was fairly sure that he would succeed.

❧

Kliwon hadn't been around the barracks the entire day. He wasn't there in the morning to help Freddie cook or in the afternoon to take the food out to the embankment where the detainees were working. He wasn't even there after roll call to help dish up the evening meal. During their month and a half in Taratakbuluh, Kliwon had done this four or five times. No one questioned him on his comings or goings because he wasn't actually a member of the group. He had been attached to the group at the last moment at the special request of Major Shinji.

At around eleven o'clock in the morning, Kliwon crossed the bridge over the river, turned left, walked through the village, and went upstream for about one hundred meters until he arrived at the village mosque. There Paktua Hasan waited for him. In Paktua Hasan's boat were all the provisions they would need: *parang*, rope, water, food.

"You're not fasting?" Kliwon inquired of Paktua Hasan while looking around him to see if anyone was watching.

"Fasting is for show. What's important is inside here,

12

right?" Paktua returned while clapping his right hand to his chest. "Are you fasting?" Paktua Hasan asked.

Kliwon looked confused. To the people of Taratakbuluh, Kliwon gave the impression of being a good Muslim, faithful in both his prayers and fasting. Now, in front of him stood the man whom the local people called "Crazy Hasan" but whose reason for not fasting during the holy month of Ramadan seemed honest and logical.

"I have so far," Kliwon answered.

As the two men rowed upstream the mid-dry-season heat became oppressive. The water was clear but very low, and the river had narrowed to no more than fifty meters in width. The sluggish current made it easy for Hasan to row and to control the direction of the boat. Kliwon had little experience with boats but tried to give a hand by rowing at the front of the boat. In fact, he did more to hinder than to help. The dense foliage of the rubber trees that stood about fifty meters from the edge of the reed-filled river banks did nothing to decrease the heat of the sun. There was almost no wind at all and the glare of the sunlight off the water burned the men's eyes. Their only protection was the *pandan*-leaf hats they wore.

An hour into their journey, Kliwon began to take off the Japanese military clothing he wore. An hour and a half and three bends in the river later, Paktua Hasan turned the boat to cross the river. Arriving at the other side he slipped into an opening among the reeds and found his way to the shore. The two men stepped out of the boat and after mooring it, sat down to rest in the shade of the rubber trees.

The site marked the border between the village-owned estate and the jungle. The jungle, unaltered by human hands, was visible to the west—virgin stands of soaring trees, each and every bit of available space filled by climbing vines, and an almost endless range of plant life. Here in the rubber estate were only row upon row of rubber trees and ground moss that unfolded around the men like a green carpet. Three and a half years of Japanese occupation had effectively killed the area's rubber industry and now the jungle was beginning to attack the edges of the estate. Because no one was tapping the rubber, the jungle would soon reclaim those areas that had once been wrested from it by force.

Although Kliwon would have preferred to rest a little while longer, Paktua Hasan exhorted him to continue their journey. They walked in snakelike fashion beneath the shade of the rubber trees, their feet cooled by the green moss. Earlier, in the boat beneath the blazing heat of the sun, Kliwon had had little desire to talk but now, in the shade of the trees, he felt his strength come back and his mind begin to focus.

"Do you travel these parts often?" he asked Paktua Hasan.

"Used to, when the Dutch were still here. I'd come two or three times a year, but not during the rainy season." In his few conversations with Paktua Hasan at Haji Zen's home and in the market, Kliwon had learned a good deal about the man's travels. One thing he learned was that about three days from Taratakbuluh was an isolated village that few outsiders had ever been to. Paktua Hasan was the only person he knew to have gone there and returned. On his trips to this village he took with him salt, matches, and simple tools like knives and *parang* but he returned with elephant tusks. Supposedly, at one time or another, a number of other villagers had gone with him to the village but they had never returned. If that were true it was odd that the people of the village and the families of these people had never asked Paktua Hasan to account for their whereabouts.

"Do the people in that village look like us?" Kliwon asked.

"Yes, but they tend to be a little smaller."

Kliwon himself wasn't a very large man but Paktua Hasan was very small. At full height he came only to Kliwon's ears, but his hands were large and muscular. A chill ran down Kliwon's spine as he thought about something he dared not mention.

"Have any of the people from that village ever visited Taratakbuluh?" Kliwon inquired.

Paktua Hasan appeared not to have heard the question because without answering it he began to speak. "There are about one hundred people living there including men, women, and children. They are good people. There's no fighting or stealing or any other kind of crime. They live in peace and help one another hunt and farm. There's no greed because everything is communally owned."

Kliwon interrupted. "What about what people say? That men who have gone there have never returned?"

"If so it's because they had sex with the women there," Paktua Hasan answered briefly.

"So they were forced to marry and stay there?"

"No, there's no force there. No force at all. A man may have sex with any woman he wishes but if he does he may never leave."

"Does a man have to marry the woman he has sex with?" The subject had begun to interest Kliwon.

"There are no married couples," Paktua Hasan replied. "The adult males are the husbands of the adult females and there is no jealousy or hurt feelings. There is no rape either. You cannot force a woman to have sex there."

"I'm afraid, Pak Hasan," Kliwon said.

"If you and the Dutch are being honest and really do want to escape from the torture of the Japanese, the people there will accept you without reservation and will guarantee your safety. As long as you leave the women alone, I guarantee that you will be able to leave the place safely at whatever time you want."

Kliwon felt somewhat relieved.

A half hour passed and the two men arrived at the edge of a swamp that appeared to stretch out almost in line with the river from which they had just come.

"My grandfather told me that the Kampar Kanan River used to flow through here," Paktua Hasan explained.

They stopped at the base of what looked like a bridge across the swamp. Kliwon observed that the bridge was

15

made from tree trunks abo·it seven meters in length. The base of the first trunk rested on the harder ground at the edge of the swamp while its other end, stretching out into the marsh, lay nestled in the crook of a diagonal cross that was embedded deep in marshy soil. The base of another tree trunk rested on the same cross and stretched out farther into the swamp, its other end almost completely hidden by the dense brush.

"There are four trunks to the other side," Paktua Hasan commented when seeing Kliwon studying the bridge.

They sat down on a fallen branch and Paktua Hasan opened his bundle of provisions.

"Go ahead and eat," he said to Kliwon.

"But what about Haji Zen? I'd be ashamed," Kliwon told him.

"He'll never find out," Paktua Hasan said with certainty. The men ate.

"With a path through this brush it will take you only about a half hour to reach the Dutch camp," Paktua Hasan informed Kliwon as they were eating. The old man pointed eastward with his hand.

"Once we've finished eating I suppose we should start cutting brush," Kliwon said with a question in his voice.

"No. I'll take care of that. The job should be finished by tomorrow night and the place passable. What we have to do today is clear away the brush from the bridge across the swamp. Some parts, you can't get across. After that we'll string some rope between the tops of those crosses for a rail."

Later, when they were working, Kliwon asked: "What about wild animals, Pak Hasan? There must be lots of tigers and snakes around here."

Paktua Hasan looked at the young man for a moment.

"Trust me," he said. "If you follow me and listen to what I say no one will get hurt. Don't anyone try to cross me or force me to do something I don't want to do," he advised.

The two men continued their work, stopping every now and then to chase away the swarms of mosquitoes that gathered around them. Kliwon counted the tree trunks. Four, together stretching more than thirty meters. The surface of the water below was invisible, completely hidden by the dense brush. Kliwon thought about the water and mud he knew must be below and asked himself how the tree trunks had ever been placed there. He kept his thoughts to himself. Across the bridge he could see a footpath whose entrance was almost hidden by hanging vines. He shivered.

By six o'clock that evening the two men had finished their work and set off on their journey home, retracing the path they had followed earlier. Finding their boat they rowed downstream at a much faster speed than had been possible on the trip upstream. They were back in Taratakbuluh by the time most villagers were preparing to break their fast.

❀

Haji Zen was the richest and most respected man in Taratakbuluh. Oddly enough, though he was native to the village, most of the people thought of him as an outsider. More than anything else this was due to the man's orientation toward Singapore, now called Shonanto by the Japanese. From the time he was a young man, Haji Zen nurtured and increased the wealth his father had left him by marketing rubber in Singapore. In his younger days he himself rafted the rubber his estate produced downstream to a village on an island near the mouth of the Kampar Kanan River. From there he took the rubber by barge to Singapore.

His wife was from Taratakbuluh too but Haji Zen—who had made the pilgrimage to Mecca twice already—hadn't married any of his children to local people. His three married daughters lived in Singapore, just as did his married son. His other son was in Singapore too, having been sent there just a few months before the arrival of the Japanese to work as an apprentice to Said Mubarak, a successful trader. Though he hadn't received any news from his five children in Singapore since the Japanese invasion, he was fairly certain they were safe. Each of them had been blessed with enough strength and independence to overcome whatever difficulties arose.

Left at home was Lena, his youngest daughter who was now nineteen years old. Most girls Lena's age had babies at their breasts. Some by that age had even lost children but Lena was still unmarried. There were two reasons for this, the first one being that Haji Zen had little desire to marry his daughter to any of the young men from the village, all of whom he thought were lazy and without sufficient desire to get ahead. The second reason was that the young men themselves were afraid to approach her.

When prior to the outbreak of the war Haji Zen had placed the care of his second son in the hands of Said Mubarak in Singapore it wasn't only his son he was thinking about. With his son at Said Mubarak's home it would be easy to arrange for Lena to meet Umar, Said Mubarak's son. What could make a *haji* like himself happier than an Arab son-in-law who was also a wealthy merchant? Now the hopes of this happening had faded. Nonetheless, he still wasn't keen on accepting one of the younger men in the village as his son-in-law. What was he to do with Lena? She was far from unattractive but was still living at home, an old maid, the butt of village gossip.

Haji Zen sought honesty and determination in a man. He had exercised great care in the selection of his children's marriage partners and taken all the time necessary to find people with the traits he admired. His caution had succeeded in giving him an abundance of wealth; the three and a half years of Japanese occupation had made no apparent impact on his life.

The same traits that he sought in in-laws he had seen in Paktua Hasan on their first meeting almost fifteen years earlier. Haji Zen had been to Mecca but once at that time. On the day of their meeting, he was busy overseeing the loading of his rubber on bamboo rafts for transport downriver. He had five men working for him and he was constantly busy telling them where to stack the sheets of rubber, how to stack them so as not to upset the balance of the raft, how much space to leave for steering, where to leave a place for sleeping. With four rafts to load he couldn't pay attention to everything at once so it wasn't until midday that he finally noticed there were six men, not five, working for him.

"Who are you?" he asked the newcomer who appeared to be somewhat older than the other men.

"My name is Hasan, Pak Haji."

"Where are you from?"

"From Sungai Pagar."

"What are you doing here?"

At that time Sungai Pagar seemed to be a long distance away. Moreover, it wasn't customary for a person from one village to look for work in another.

"I was with a group of ivory hunters but got lost and ended up here."

"When did you arrive?" Haji Zen asked somewhat suspiciously.

"This morning, Pak Haji," Hasan answered in a patient and respectful tone of voice.

"What are you doing here? Trying to earn enough money to go home?"

"If I can find a steady job, I won't go home. Even in Sungai Pagar I'm an outsider. I have no family and no permanent place to live."

"Why didn't you say something before you started working?"

"I didn't have anything to do so I didn't think there would be any problem helping out. Is that so wrong?" Hasan turned the question around.

The logic of the man's statement and the simplicity of his question touched something inside Haji Zen. Still he remained somewhat suspicious of Hasan and looked at him more closely. Haji Zen was one of the *silat* champions in the village and felt no physical fear of the man. There was something much stronger than curiosity that piqued his interest in finding out more about the man. The man who called himself Hasan had an honest face. "Just like an open book," Haji Zen told his wife later, and though he wasn't a large man Hasan's well-muscled body was evidence that he was accustomed to working hard.

Hasan went along with Haji Zen to Singapore but that was the only trip they made together. Hasan said that he preferred to hunt for ivory and, in fact, every time he went into the jungle he came back carrying elephant tusks. Gradually the employer-employee relationship that once existed between the two men changed to one of fellow traders. Later it became even closer when Haji Zen's children began to treat Hasan as part of the family.

For years Paktua Hasan slept beneath the overhang of Haji Usman's *warung*. He never married and was always around when people needed help. He offered his assistance with no thought of recompense and was such a good man that people in the village began to think of him as crazy or at least a little crazy. Everyone liked him but he, for his part, seemed oblivious to all that went on around him. Fifteen years later Hasan looked the same as he did the day Haji Zen met him. Haji Zen looked older.

Haji Zen came to know a great deal about the ways and means of Hasan's life and about the village where Hasan obtained ivory by trading for it with inexpensive items. Haji Zen placed his full trust in Hasan. When Hasan and Kliwon came to him saying they intended to help the detainees escape, Haji Zen not only agreed with their plan; he also promised to provide whatever provisions they would need for their journey. There was only one question that bothered him about the proposition: why did Kliwon have to flee?

After breaking fast and performing *magrib* prayers on Tuesday evening in mid August, 2605, Haji Zen decided to put his question to Kliwon. The young man had arrived at the house just as he and his family were about to break fast. There was still time for Kliwon to bathe. Finding a sarong to wear was no problem. At Haji Zen's house there were always extra sarongs for guests but Kliwon was no longer just another guest.

20

"Why do you have to run away?" Haji Zen finally asked him. "After all, you're not an enemy and you're not a detainee of the Japanese either, are you?"

Though he tried to hide his confusion, Kliwon appeared somewhat shaken by the question. He didn't know what to say. He had thought about it for a long time and had hoped the question wouldn't arise. What was he to say? Although he did not smoke, his fingers itched for one of Haji Zen's Kooa cigarettes lying on the floor mat. But that would only make his nervousness more apparent.

"I'm afraid, Pak Haji," he answered off the top of his head, hoping that his answer would be enough to put an end to further questioning or, at the very least, give him enough time to think of a more logical answer.

"But the Japanese here aren't mean, Kliwon," commented Haji Deramah, the wife of Haji Zen. "It's not like when they were building the railway."

"But if one person disobeys their orders, everyone suffers for it, Bu Haji," Kliwon answered, beginning to feel that he had found a hold.

"If the Dutch were to escape and you were to stay, would they put you on trial?" Lena asked, not quite ready to believe him.

"I'm sure of it."

"All of the Dutch are going to escape," he answered confidently even though he wasn't sure they all would. The detainees always spoke in Dutch when discussing their escape plans.

"But you could hide here in Taratakbuluh," Haji Zen insisted. "We could hide you in one of the fish-trapping places along the streams that run into the Kampar Kanan. There are thousands of them. You wouldn't have to worry about being found out."

"Let the Dutch go off alone with Paktua," Lena suggested.

"But if I were discovered, everyone in the village would have to pay the consequences," Kliwon countered.

21

Nothing was said for a moment and then Haji Zen asked slowly, "How long would you stay in the jungle?"

"I'm not sure about the Dutch, Pak Haji," Kliwon answered. "But, for myself, when I think it's safe and the Japanese have calmed down, I'll come back immediately."

"Do you think the Japanese will do anything to the people here in the village?" Haji Zen inquired.

"I don't think so. We won't be making our escape through the village."

"When do you intend to try?"

"As soon as possible, Pak Haji. Maybe tomorrow; we're ready. Pak Hasan promised that he would clear a path from the camp to the crossing point and that he would be finished by tomorrow."

Lena looked as if she wanted to say something but then didn't. Haji Zen could see it in her eyes. He had guessed some time ago that Lena had placed her hopes of marriage on Kliwon. Was that so strange? If not on Kliwon, then whom? Most of the men in the village of Lena's age were married. Besides, there wasn't a reliable one among them and not one of them had the nerve to approach Lena anyway.

Haji Zen was aware that Kliwon was not ideal but then, with the world as it was, was there anyone around who could meet his standards? Once there had been, he mused, as his thoughts flew back to Said Mubarak's son in Singapore. The light in Umar's eyes showed intelligence and a deep-seated desire to advance and become rich. But, as the saying went, if the rattan has been taken then you must make do with its roots.

His family had always been able to stand above all difficulties. Could Kliwon maintain—he need not raise—the standing of his family? Could this young man be entrusted with the care of his estate, his large home, and all the expensive furnishings he had purchased in Singapore before the war? He had brought in a select group of workmen from Singapore to build this large home of his and almost all the items in it were from Singapore too. Neither Haji Deramah nor Lena had ever learned how to sew on a machine but he had a new and yet untouched Singer. Then there was the Italian marble table and the Gramophone with a collection of Abdul Wahab and Umi Kaltsum records. It was too bad he had no needles for the machine or, for that matter, kerosene to fill the new and unused Petromax lamps. But that didn't really matter. These were symbols of his family's pride, representations of what he always said was "the sap of the tree but not the tree itself."

Could Kliwon take care of all this? Haji Zen was somewhat skeptical and to himself he admitted that the young man's plans of escape came as a hidden blessing.

Shortly before ten o'clock Haji Zen's family set out from the house. Haji Zen felt very satisfied as he walked with his family toward the mosque where they would join with other villagers in *tarawih*, the voluntary prayers held during the fasting month. With a bundle of food supplies in his hands for *sahur*, the postmidnight meal that precedes a day of fasting, Kliwon felt satisfied too as he walked back to the camp across the wooden railroad trestle that connected the two banks of the Kampar Kanan River.

❖

When ordered to surround the three motion picture halls in Bukittinggi one night in mid April, 2604, the Dai Nippon soldiers were given simple instructions: round up all men not carrying identification papers. They need only be above eighteen years of age and in relatively good health. The soldiers were not to take men whose wives were with them or men who worked as civil servants or in the offices of the Dai Nippon occupation government. That is how Anis had been caught.

Anis, twenty-one years old at the time, was a *babelok*, a traveling merchant who bought and sold anything that might turn a profit. At one time or another, almost every adult Minangkabau male tries the life of a *babelok* which by many is seen as carefree and unfettered. Some men worked as *babelok* until age alone forced them to stop. With two or three wives, each of them living at a different place along his route, the life of a *babelok* couldn't be said to be all bad. There was not a *ranah*, one of the low-lying valleys that mark the geography of the Minangkabau region, that was not traversed by hundreds of groups of *babelok* every day. Nonetheless, the groups themselves were like grains of sand on a beach with no real adhesion among them. Each *babelok* was his own king with full control over the decisions he made. Two or three brothers or relatives might form a *kongsi*, a loose commercial association, but these rarely lasted very long.

On that unfortunate night Anis had been at the cinema with Ujang, his thirteen-year-old brother who had begun traveling with Anis a year earlier after finishing primary school in their home village.

"Now what kind of work do they have planned for us?" Anis complained bitterly to Ujang.

"Maybe there's a bridge down. It shouldn't take too long," Ujang consoled.

This kind of forced labor had become customary in the region. Usually the men who were rounded up were forced to work for four or five days. They were given sufficient food so the work was not in fact an excessive burden for the local populace. Moreover, the work the men were forced to do was usually of direct benefit to the area: reconstruction of a fallen bridge, the clearing of roads after landslides, and so on.

"Hold on to this money," Anis ordered his brother as he handed him a wad of bills and some handwritten IOUs. "Settle my debts and then wait for me at home."

That night Anis and the other men who had been caught were taken to Payakumbuh. There they stayed overnight with hundreds of other men who apparently had been rounded up in other cities of the region. Early the next morning the men were transported by a slow-moving convoy of trucks to Pakanbaru. On the third day they were taken by train to Lipat Kain and on the fourth day they were hard at work with Dutch detainees and Javanese *romusha* on the construction of a railway toward Sijunjung in the southwest, the site of the terminal for coal coming from Sawah Lunto.

The Minangkabau people make poor laborers and most are too clever to be caught doing forced labor for an extended period of time. Furthermore, because at the site where Anis was working there were too many laborers and too little food, the Japanese guards did not keep a close eye on the workers. By the time 1944 ended not a single one of the Minangkabau workers remained. One rainy afternoon in November Anis calmly boarded a cargo train and by evening was in Pakanbaru.

The strong sense of socialism and *gotong royong* of the Minangkabau people is apparent in numerous proverbs that act as their guidelines for a proper way of life. Their equally strong sense of individualism, however, is rarely expressed in metaphorical phrases; when it is, it might be in a phrase such as "In this world, the only friend you have is yourself; everyone else is an enemy." It is these two contradictory world views that produce in the Minangkabau people a strong sense of self-confidence and caution and, at the same time, kindle the tradition of *merantau*, whereby a young man is expected to leave his village and find success outside before he is accepted as an adult at home. This tradition had been one factor in the maturation of Anis but another equally important factor was the time he spent hacking away at the virgin jungle of Sumatra alongside the Javanese *romusha* and the Dutch detainees in constant accompaniment with hardship and death.

With the help of people from his home village who lived in Pakanbaru, Anis collected enough money to return home, but what he found there differed significantly from the image that had nourished his hopes for the future during his months of suffering. After only a few days at home he returned to Pakanbaru to begin a new *babelok* business from scratch. Now every Tuesday he could be found on the train to Taratakbuluh where on market day he would sell the goods he carried with him and purchase smoked fish. That same evening he would return to Pakanbaru and on Thursday would sell his fish either wholesale or retail at Batu Satu Market. On Friday he would make a similar trip to Sungai Pagar from whence he would return on Saturday. His enterprise piqued the interest of other Minang traders and now there were about ten *babelok* whose livelihood depended on the coal train that chugged its way through the Sumatra jungle.

The footpath that went upstream from the railroad embankment followed the Kampar Kanan's northern bank, heavily overgrown with reeds. The path led directly to a small mosque where the villagers held their Friday prayers, where those without work to do spent their time, and where in the evenings the village children learned to recite the Quran. The path was about three hundred meters long and the first house visible on it was the home of Haji Zen. Twenty or thirty meters beyond Haji Zen's home was an open field, about fifty by one hundred meters in size, where the children of the village played soccer and which on Wednesdays was used as an open-air market. Beyond the field was a two-story wooden structure that served as Haji Usman's home, a *warung*, and a store for everyday needs. To the left of it stood a row of smaller homes made of wood and woven split bamboo.

The Minang traders lodged with Haji Usman. They stayed on the second floor of the dark-colored building. Haji Usman lived on the lower level, the same level as the food stall and store. For the Minang traders, it was almost like a small party as they broke fast on that Tuesday evening, August 14, 2605. This was the sixth day of the fasting month but the first day they had broken fast in Taratakbuluh, and Haji Usman didn't let the opportunity slip by to earn a little extra income for himself. After *magrib* prayers and the breaking of fast, the inhabitants of Haji Usman's food stall, boardinghouse, and home proceeded to the mosque for *isa* prayers and *tarawih*. Haji Usman was about to join them but Anis held him back, saying that he would like to talk with him about something.

Except for the flickering palm oil lamp on the table in the food stall where the two men sat, the place was pitch black. Outside, villagers with torches in their hands passed by on the way to the mosque. Every now and then the two men would have to interrupt their conversation to reply, "You go on ahead, we'll be along shortly."

Haji Usman slowly rolled a thatch palm cigarette. Putting it to the lamp flame, he drew in the smoke deeply and tried to guess what it was the young man sitting before him wanted to talk about.

Anis opened the conversation with a straightforward question: "Is Haji Zen's daughter engaged to be married, Pak Haji?"

Haji Usman was startled awake from his daydreaming. He looked at the young man. Anis was somewhat different from the other Minang traders. He maintained an air of calm, had little use for false praise or friendship, and was both open and modest as well. Whenever Anis came to Taratakbuluh he brought him something, a "token of friendship" so he said, for which Haji Usman was most appreciative. That evening, for example, Anis had given him four boxes of matches, a rare commodity during the Japanese occupation. Anis had told him, "So that your wife will have an easier time lighting the fire to prepare *sahur*," but Haji Usman had ordered his wife to put away the matches for use in times of real emergency. For their daily needs, a flintstone, a metal striker, and a little thatch for tinder were sufficient. with the exception of Haji Zen, that is how everyone in the village started their fires. Was there a hidden motive behind this young man's gifts? But then, so what if there were?

"As far as I know, Lena is not engaged, but, Anis, I think you should keep in mind that Haji Zen's daughter is of a slightly different class." Haji Usman was trying not to be too pessimistic. "If it's a wife you want, why not someone else? There are lots of young girls around here, all of them much easier than Lena to obtain. And younger too. What with the marriage standards of this village, Lena will have a difficult time finding a husband. The most she can hope for is a widower."

"So then, if I propose I just might be accepted," Anis answered immediately.

"You might have something there," Haji Usman replied after thinking about it for a moment.

"Would you be willing to help me?" Anis asked.

How could he not say yes to the young man's request? Haji Usman wondered. But how could he talk about this matter with Haji Zen? Haji Zen was not a man given to small talk or beating around the bush, and Haji Usman's relationship with him, much like that of everyone else in the village, was akin to the relationship between a commoner and a friend of the king. Even Pak Lurah, the village chief, Pak Khatib, the religious leader, and Tuan Kadhi, the local record keeper, deferred to Haji Zen and heeded his advice in most every matter.

"All right," Haji Usman said at last. "I will help you but I advise you to prepare yourself. Here, in this village a girl's family often makes numerous demands. I don't want you to embarrass me."

"I think that it would be best to be frank from the start and tell him directly what we want. I have no family. I'm completely alone and everything I have is what I use for trading capital."

"With Haji Zen, being frank might be the best way," Haji Usman commented after saying nothing for a moment.

Haji Usman's four children were married. When his only son had decided to marry, his brother-in-law had helped with the proposal. His brother-in-law had also been there to give the official reply when his daughters were proposed to. He himself had often attended such ceremonies but had never acted as a go-between. What would he say? How was he to begin? He would think about that later.

Passing by on the road along the river were Haji Zen, Haji

28

Deramah, and Lena. Haji Zen walked in front, a torch in his hand, while his wife and daughter followed behind with prayer mats and their white, *sholat* veils.

"Who's the younger man that spends so much time at Haji Zen's house?" Anis inquired of Haji Usman.

Well, well, Haji Usman thought. Apparently Anis had spent some time watching Haji Zen's house.

"Oh, him," he answered nonchalantly. "Just a Javanese *romusha*. His name is Kliwon. He often helps out at Haji Zen's house but he lives in the barracks across the river."

"Does he come by every day?"

"Seems to, but that's more of a coincidence that anything. Haji Zen's having him put in a vegetable garden behind the house. Don't know if it will work. No one around here has ever tried it before. But you don't have to worry about him. From what Crazy Hasan's told me, the men in the camp are planning to escape into the jungle."

From the direction of the mosque came the sound of the muezzin's cry, calling people to *isa* prayers. The two men set off for the mosque in haste and arrived there just as the *gomat*, the second call to prayer, ended. They stood in the row near the screen of muslin cloth that demarcated the women's place of prayer.

After the completion of *isa* prayers and *tarawih*, Haji Usman and Anis took their time in leaving, hoping to be on the road at the same time as Haji Zen. Lena, like the rest of the girls of the village, stayed behind, intending to stop at friends' homes before going to bed. Most of the young men remained in the mosque for *tadarusan*, taking turns reciting passages of the Quran until it was time for *sahur*.

"*Assalamu'alaikum*, Pak Haji," Haji Usman said while extending his hand in greetng to Haji Zen.

"*Wa'alaikum salam*," he replied immediately as he took Haji Usman's hand. He then extended his hand to Anis.

"This is Anis, Pak Haji," Haji Usman said in introduction. "Anis is one of the *babelok* who lodge at my house."

"Yes, I've seen him here before," Haji Zen commented. "There are about ten of you, aren't there?" he asked Anis.

"Yes, there are about ten in the group but not everyone comes every time," Anis answered respectfully.

"I suppose they're rich enough that they don't have to," Haji Zen jested and laughed.

"Come now, Pak Haji. Traders like us never have money."

"You'll have to stop by the house some time," Haji Zen said politely.

"Thank you for the invitation, Pak Haji. I hope that we will be able to stop by."

"Would you like to break fast at my house next Tuesday?"

"God willing, Pak Haji."

❁

Plans for the construction of a railroad from Pakanbaru in Riau to Sijunjung in west Sumatra had apparently been drawn up by the Japanese long before the outbreak of the Pacific War. Within a few months after their occupation of Indonesia, the Japanese had gathered together a large number of Dutch detainees and Javanese *romusha* in Pakanbaru to begin work on the railway. Meanwhile, all nonvital railway lines in north Sumatra, west Sumatra, south Sumatra, and Java were dismantled and shipped by barge to Pakanbaru, the river port located deep in the heart of Sumatra. A few months later locomotives and cargo cars were brought in. Then began the clearing of jungle tracts and construction of a railroad in a way that had never been tried before. Rivers, both large and small, were spanned by wooden trestles which the trains passed over only with extreme caution. Marshes were drained but only enough to allow railroad ties to be laid. Without a firm foundation it wasn't long before the railway collapsed, but that only meant the marsh was drained once more and the rails relaid. Tracks were laid around mountains, not through them, and sometimes at such an incline that locomotives rarely had the power to make the climb in one try and would be forced to back up and wait to build up sufficient steam to continue the journey.

A great number of the Dutch internees and *romusha* died

in the construction of that railroad. Some from accidents, others because of hunger, malaria, torture, or a combination of all of these. The reasons behind their deaths were unimportant but the number of men who died and were used to shore up the foundation of the tracks will never be known. Stories about the railroad and its construction say that for every railroad tie one man gave his life. As for the railroad trestles, the number of lives that were lost in their construction could be determined by the size of the bridge.

Only a few months after the beginning of 2605, coal was already being transported from the collection point in Sijunjung to Pakanbaru. From that harbor city thrust hundreds of kilometers into the heart of Sumatra, the coal was carried by barge to another location and out of the jurisdiction of the commander of the Riau Regional Military Authority whose offices were located in Pakanbaru. This, however, did not mean the end of headaches for the regional military commander. He had thousands of problems to deal with, each one more important, more urgent, more pressing than the other: how to keep the wheels of government and the economy of this region of almost one million people moving; how to provide food for the thousands of Japanese soldiers, Dutch prisoners, and Indonesian *romusha*; how to achieve the targets that had been set for the region. The list went on.

The officer in charge of railroad communications was responsible for finding solutions to the last problem which in itself encompassed thousands of other problems: how to make sure that the railroad was completed on time and that the coal was kept flowing at a fast pace to Pakanbaru (requesting more *romusha* from Java would be difficult—more workers would have to be "recruited" in the Riau area); how to feed the huge number of workers (sago was turned into dried noodles); how to keep the work force from being decimated by malaria (give each man one quinine tablet per day); how to keep the completed railroad safe from danger (a special team was formed to deal with this problem).

According to the information that made its way to Riau,

31

the course of the Greater East Asian War had changed direction and was now striking Japan. Allied bombers were dropping their loads unchecked and the periodic communiqués that the district commanders received gave neither hope nor encouragement on how the war was to end. Real news was becoming more deeply buried beneath slogans and orders to keep up one's spirit. There were targets to realize and duties to fulfill. At the local level, none of the commanders wanted to be seen as a factor in the defeat of Japan—that is, of course, if the Japanese were defeated.

Ose's thoughts moved over these and other problems as he sat inside the security post waiting for the promised telephone call from headquarters. He felt that he knew the root of the problem. Supposing that from the beginning he had followed in Shinji's footsteps and danced to the beating of the drum he might now hold the same position and rank as Shinji, possibly an even higher one. He too was a technical school graduate and had begun his military career with the rank of second lieutenant, but it had taken six years before he had make the rank of first lieutenant. And that was more than three years ago! In a large war, advancement at such a slow speed was a slap on the cheek.

The security post was in fact the front porch of the barracks in which the ten Japanese soldiers in Ose's charge lived. The corner beams of the building with its woven bamboo walls and tar paper roof were rubber trees. The security post measured the distance between two trees by the distance between another two trees. Its bamboo walls were eighty decimeters high. An opening in one of the walls served as a doorway to the outside, another as a doorway to the soldiers' barracks. The table inside the post was made of two wooden planks. Three of the table's legs were planted in the ground. The fourth leg was the rubber tree that supported the righthand corner of the post. The long bench behind the table was another plank sitting on two poles that had been driven in the ground.

Atop the table sat a telephone whose hookup was a simple piece of wire that ran from headquarters to Sijunjung in the far southwest. Because of the simplicity of the phone system, any call that was made on the line would set the telephone of each and every post ringing. For that reason, each post was assigned a calling code made up of long rings (dial twice) and short rings (dial once). The code for Taratakbuluh, for example, was one long, two shorts, one long. The call that Ose was now waiting for was one for all posts, a special number—three shorts—that would be repeated until all parties on the line had answered.

Ose listened to the sound from the piece of rail that hung in front of the security post as it was struck ten times. It was 10 P.M., Tokyo time. Still the call hadn't come. A man with a torch was visible on the bridge. The flame appeared to flicker and die as the man moved in and out of sight behind the rubber trees that partially obstructed Ose's view. For a moment the man stood poised on the embankment that was under repair, then the flame swooped down the slope and moved in the direction of the camp.

It was Kliwon. He looked surprised to see Ose at the security post. Moving toward him quickly, Kliwon stopped at a distance of four or five meters where he pulled his body erect, bowed slightly at the waist, and said *"Konban-wa,"* about the only Japanese greeting he knew.

"Where have you been all day?" Ose asked in Indonesian.

Ose liked speaking Indonesian and used it whenever he had the chance. For this ability he was extremely thankful to Anwar-san, the teacher at the primary school that stood in front of the resident's office in Pakanbaru. The young unmarried teacher stopped by almost every evening to give him a lesson apparently with no thought of recompense whatsoever. To honor Anwar-san's service to him, Ose now used Bahasa Indonesia with every Indonesian he met.

"I was sleeping in the mosque, Masta," Kliwon answered.

"Sleeping?"

"I'm fasting, Masta. I don't eat all day and I feel dizzy."

"Did you sleep yesterday?'

"Yesterday I still felt strong, Masta."

Ose wanted to ask him to stop fasting, but didn't. He

knew that Kliwon was lying. Only a liar could act so convincingly. A good-for-nothing, that's what Ose thought of Kliwon, but what harm was he doing to the barracks?

"Have you eaten?" Ose inquired.

"Yes, Masta. I eat with the people in the village."

"All right, you may go," Ose ordered.

Kliwon saluted and then proceeded toward the detainees' barracks where he slept.

Shinji, or Major Shinji now. They had become friends at the technical school in Osaka. Shinji had always been protective of him. He too had begun his military career at the rank of second lieutenant but he was now on the staff of the Railroad Communications Command Force. It was Shinji who had given him the opportunity to be a commander and it was Shinji who on Sunday, July 1, one and a half months ago, when Ose and his men were boarding the train for their trip to Taratakbuluh, had come to the station with Kliwon who carried a parcel in his hand.

"Ose-san," Shinji had said, "take this man with you. His job here was to carry water for the barracks. You can have him do anything."

"Well, if you don't need him any longer, why don't you let him go like the rest?"

At this question Shinji burst into laughter. "He's in danger," he answered. "There have been people waiting for him outside the barracks for days now and he doesn't have the courage to leave."

"What did he do?"

"He was caught fooling around with the wife of the owner of the *warung* in front of the barracks."

Ose took him in.

When thinking about it, he saw that the help Shinji gave him was often for Shinji's personal interests. Shinji had invited him to study *sumo* at the temple of Priest Ando, now his father-in-law. (Could he still call the man his father-in-law after what Michiko had done?) But, in the end, it was only Ose who studied. Shinji spent most of his time at the temple visiting with Yoshie.

34

Michiko. His wife. If I were to die, Ose wondered, would the government send the news to Michiko at her undoubtedly small and unkempt apartment in Tokyo, the place where her lover, a high military officer, visited her? At one time Ose had stood in awe of Michiko, the young woman who patiently introduced him to the beauty and glory of Japanese traditions that had been handed down for thousands of generations. "How wonderful if we could seal our friendship by marriage to Yoshie and Michiko," Shinji had one day suggested. And that is what had happened.

But the parcel of jewels? It was difficult for Ose to understand why Shinji had given the jewels to him. "The war will be over soon and we'll return home. You might need them then," Shinji had told him when handing him the bundle. But that was three and a half years ago and still the war was not over. Moreover, if they were to return home in the near future, it would probably be as prisoners of war.

Whatever the case, Shinji was his friend, the best friend he had ever had.

Two of the soldiers on night watch began to make their rounds, replacing the torches that had been set up earlier in the evening with fresh ones. Besides the telephone, the daily log, and a list of calling codes for each of the posts and camps along the railway, there was also a clock on the table. It now showed twelve o'clock. One of the soldiers hurriedly struck the piece of rail in front of the security post twelve times.

It wasn't until the next change of torches that the telephone began to ring. Three shorts, over and over. Ose felt at once surprised, afraid, and relieved. He held his hand on the receiver a long time before slowly lifting it to his ear. At other posts the telephone continued to ring. Ring-ring-ring, ring-ring-ring . . .

"Men," the voice from headquarters began, "before we convey the news that you have been waiting for, we would like to find out if all of you can hear what is being said."

One by one the names of the post commanders were called out. The person called gave his name and rank and

35

provided a brief report on the activities as well as the condition of the security post he was in charge of. Nothing out of the ordinary had happened that day.

"Men," the voice continued after the completion of roll call, "we know that you have been waiting for this call with discipline and spirit intact. It is these two factors that helped bring glory to Dai Nippon at the outset of the Greater East Asian War. It is also these factors that have protected *Tennō Heika* and the motherland and brought us to the end of this glory-filled war. Neither reports from the battlefield nor news from the motherland can be used as a sure guide. Perhaps tomorrow we'll receive word. The commander for the Riau Military Region may be forced to make his own decisions. Regardless, you are requested to report tomorrow to the gymnasium of the residency, the home of the commander. He will convene the meeting at 2100 Tokyo time. All commanders are required to attend. Carry out your duties as you normally would and do not attract attention. Good night. *Tennō Heika, banzai!*"

"*Banzai!*" everyone answered.

Ose continued to hold the telephone receiver long after the connection had been cut. He wasn't satisfed. He didn't understand the meaning of the call but there was nothing he could do about it that night except return to his hut, eat, and sleep. He walked slowly back toward his hut. Kiguchi and the three soldiers on watch stood at attention and saluted. He heard Kiguchi's voice. "Good night, Commander."

❧

"I still don't see what use there is in running away," Pastor said after all the Dutch detainees were back in the barracks.

Wimpie had only cashew apples to eat that night and was now roasting the nuts. With apparent calm he gathered the nuts he had roasted into a rubber tapping cup and carried them to the spot where he normally slept, beside the door. All conversation in the barracks stopped. All eyes were fixed on the two men, Wimpie and the Pastor. Pastor's remark had caught their attention.

"I thought we finished our discussion about that last

36

night," Wimpie said patiently as he began to eat the cashew nuts.

"It's not finished, Wimpie. You can bet that if you escape, those who remain behind will be tortured. Would that make you happy?"

Although the men knew none of the Japanese could understand Dutch, they kept their conversation to a whisper.

"That's why I suggested that we all run away. Hell, even Kliwon wants to get out of here. And why? He's not an enemy of the Japanese."

The rest of the men continued to follow the conversation, some of them leaning against the split bamboo wall of the barracks while eating what food they had gathered earlier, others sitting on the ground around the small fire. Pastor sat on the edge of the *balai* with his legs stretched toward the fire. He looked sharply in the direction of the door but Wimpie pretended to ignore him.

"The war is almost over, Wimpie," Pastor said.

"I've been hearing that for almost a year. Every time Willie puts his ear to the cans and wires there's good news to hear. Tokyo has been bombed. Osaka's been bombed too. Hundreds of Japanese ships have been sunk, hundreds of planes downed, and thousands of soldiers dead. Almost a year now. But what's really been downed is us, Pastor, not the Japanese."

"We have to be patient. This is a big war and it's not going to be over in the bat of an eye," Pastor answered calmly.

"But we have to face the facts. You've heard for yourself what Willie calls 'radio reports,' haven't you?" Wimpie was becoming more spirited.

"Unless we can trust one another, life here is going to be hell . . ."

"Shit! It already is hell, Pastor!" Wimpie half screamed, completely cutting off Pastor's comment.

The rest of the men turned to watch Pastor, curious to know what he would say.

This same discussion had gone on for over a month and the general impression was that some kind of consensus had been reached on the issue the night before; those who wanted to escape would attempt to do so; those who didn't, would stay and bear the risk. It was up to the individual to decide whether the war was coming to an end or not. Wimpie and his group were irritated by Pastor's renewed attempt to discuss the issue. Pastor should have known from past experience that it would take more strength than he had—the Japanese, for instance—to overcome Wimpie's will. Even with the Japanese, Wimpie felt fairly sure of being able to do what he wanted.

Dem had tried putting an end to the discussion as soon as it began and the conflict of wills had subsequently developed into hatred. The former member of the Dutch swim team at the Berlin Olympiad had felt it necessary to settle their argument in an open fight, but at this Wimpie had beaten him royally. It was too bad that Lieutenant Ose had interrupted them. That didn't matter now, because two days after the incident the "accident" had taken place.

The faces of all the men in the barracks indicated remembrance of the incident. Some men looked angry, some satisfied, others acquiescent, but the general mood was that if Wimpie wanted to run away, let him. Better that than another accident.

"We have to be patient, trust in God, and ask Him for His guidance. We must help one another to lighten this burden of suffering we bear. God will rescue us in our need."

Pastor maintained a calm and steady voice. He did not seem to be emotional. Now seated crosslegged on the *balai*, he appeared to exercise great caution over his choice of words. The torch attached to the pole in the middle of the room threw its light on Pastor's face. Pastor was almost bald but had a thick mustache and beard. From the manner in which he sat and spoke one sensed that he was a man of infinite patience. He reminded Wimpie of Saint Joseph.

Marie de Wit pointed at the painting on the wall above the piano. "That's Saint Joseph," she said. "He's my favorite because he's the forgotten saint."

Marie, the adopted child of the de Wits, was a new classmate of Wimpie's at MULO, the junior high school for both

Dutch and native children. They were both in third level and Wimpie, a great fan of Max Schmeling, who had beaten Joe Louis that year, was given Marie's special attention. This pleased Wimpie immensely because it was the first time any of the girls had paid attention to him. Because of his roving hands and dirty mouth, all of the other girls in the class had learned long ago to maintain a distance from him. Had it not been for Saint Joseph, Marie might have had much more reason to regret the flattery she initially paid to Wimpie.

On his frequent visits to the de Wit family home in the Kwitang section of Batavia, Wimpie kept a close watch on the habits of Mr. and Mrs. de Wit. On that unlucky night he had slipped out of the dormitory through the window and gone to the de Wit residence, knowing that Mr. and Mrs. de Wit would be at the Club de Harmonie. When he arrived Marie was playing the piano. Her schoolbooks lay scattered atop the table.

"Naughty boy. You snuck out of the dormitory, didn't you?" Marie teased.

"No, I got permission because I wanted to see you," Wimpie replied. "Where are your mother and father?" he asked, pretending not to know.

As he spoke with Marie his eyes took in the situation around him. The curtain to the central sitting room was closed as were the shutters on the windows in the front room. The door to the dining room was open but no one was there. The door to the kitchen and the servants' quarters was shut.

"They're at the club. Sit down, they won't be gone long," the young woman answered.

Wimpie did not waste much time. He approached the girl from behind, embraced her and bore his lips into the nape of her neck while his hands moved upward toward her breasts. The girl squirmed and twisted her body around. She gave him her lips but then Wimpie's hands began inching their way downward. Marie began to protest but Wimpie forced her backward against the wall.

"Don't, Wimpie—Saint Joseph," the girl cried softly

while pointing at the painting on the wall. The hapless girl assumed that Wimpie would go no further.

Wimpie paid no attention to Marie's protest and now began his attack in earnest. Marie screamed and hit Wimpie in the face with the music book she was holding in her hands. She then grabbed for the candelabra on the piano and brought that down on the young man's head. Wimpie dropped his hold. Marie turned to run but fell against the wall. As she fell her hands clutched at the painting of Saint Joseph which she tore free from its nail. Wimpie rushed toward her and Marie, swinging the painting of Saint Joseph as hard as she could, brought it down on Wimpie's head. The sharp edge of picture frame tore into Wimpie's cheek. At last alerted by the commotion inside the house, the servants came running in from the back.

The following day Wimpie was kicked out of the dormitory and dismissed from school. This time Mr. Adams, Wimpie's father, did not come to the defense of his son. Nonetheless, from his home in Bogor he continued to send Wimpie his allowance and with that money Wimpie took up lodgings at the home of Mr. Van den Broek, the boxing trainer at the Dutch garrison.

With his eyes on Pastor like a cat watching a mouse, Wimpie tried to guess how many seconds Pastor would be able to defend himself if he were attacked. Dem had held out for quite some time, five minutes at least; falling back, looking for a chance to strike, falling back again as he continued to track him. Falling back, falling back again, almost a hundred meters. By the time Lieutenant Ose saved him, his face was a mess of black and blue. Dem had been a good opponent, Wimpie thought with some admiration.

"Does God teach us to be afraid?" Wimpie asked.

"No, God does not teach us to be afraid, Wimpie. But what you're planning on doing is not an action of courage."

"Then what's your definition of courage?" Wimpie retorted.

Van Roscott ignored the question and continued his argument. "What you're planning is unreasonable and foolish. A bunch of half-starved Dutch prisoners are no match for the Sumatran jungle."

"We have Kliwon and Paktua Hasan to show the way," Wimpie remarked derisively.

"Have you ever met this Hasan?" Pastor asked.

"Freddie has, haven't you, Freddie?" Wimpie said as he motioned toward the cook. "What did you think of him?"

Freddie seemed reluctant to be brought into the conversation. His answer was fairly noncommittal: "Oh, nothing out of the ordinary. Just like other natives."

Freddie's answer enraged Wimpie but he held his anger in check. He couldn't afford to make too many enemies. His instincts cautioned him on that.

"Besides, Wimpie, you have no idea what the man is really like inside," Pastor said in a monotone but with a touch of irritation in his voice.

"Piss on the natives. I've been with locals since I was a kid, Pastor. The first woman I had was a native woman. Who says I don't know what they're like inside?" Wimpie's real feelings were beginning to show.

The woman Wimpie spoke of was his mother's servant. Wimpie had been only eleven at the time. What was her name? He couldn't remember. The first time he had her the woman's husband, the family's gardener, was still working for them. The next day the man had asked permission to resign and then had left, not taking his wife with him. She continued to work for the Adams family. Mr. Adams, the administrator of the tea plantation outside Bogor, never found out why the gardener resigned. As for Mrs. Adams, she one day remarked to her servant: "I think your husband's taken another wife. Sundanese men are simply no good!"

"For three and a half years this country has been occupied by Japan. We have no idea what the Japanese have taught them," Pastor argued, unwilling to give in.

"They're all the same, no better than slaves who will always choose the better master. The Japanese have brought only suffering. The natives are sure to want us back."

From outside came the sound of Lieutenant Ose's voice

and then Kliwon's greeting. A little while later, the native man entered the barracks but paused in the doorway when he saw that the Dutch were still awake. Now what's going on? he wondered, as he made his way to the corner on the opposite side of the room from where Wimpie slept.

❀

Wimpie rose and walked toward the fire.

"Come over here, Kliwon," he ordered in Bahasa Indonesia.

Tired from his day's journey, Kliwon hadn't even been allowed the opportunity to lie down and stretch his legs. But, afraid of Wimpie, he did as ordered. Wimpie knew what had happened in Pakanbaru and why he had been forced to flee to Taratakbuluh. Another, simpler reason for obeying was that Wimpie was a boxer and even three and a half years in detention with its hard work and poor food had not diminished his strength. Kliwon had seen with his own eyes what had happened to Dem and how he had been beaten. But what frightened Kliwon most about Wimpie was the extremely coarse and rude nature of his talk and behavior.

Kliwon moved slowly from the *balai* and walked toward the fire. He felt nervous with so many eyes on him and more than slightly uncomfortable having been brought into the middle of an argument. What else could it be? Although none of the men had said anything since he entered the barracks, he could feel the tension in the air. He cursed himself for ever opening his big mouth and telling Wimpie of his affair with Kak Siti.

"When can we get the hell out of this godforsaken place?" Wimpie asked him no sooner than he had sat down on a piece of wood. Wimpie spoke slowly in Indonesian, almost whispering as he motioned Kliwon toward the middle of the room. This precaution was necessary because Lieutenant Ose, if none of the other Japanese soldiers, could understand Indonesian.

Kliwon felt tongue-tied, especially so when the Dutch

began to form a circle around him. At the same time, he felt somewhat relieved as well because it appeared he wasn't being made part of a fight.

"Tomorrow night if you want," he answered cautiously.

"What's been done? Where's the escape route? What preparations have been made? What about food in the jungle? How are we supposed to fend off tigers and snakes?" Wimpie shot off his questions in nonstop succession.

Kliwon replied quickly, hoping to prevent Wimpie from becoming angry with him. "Pak Hasan has guaranteed everything," he said.

"What kind of guarantee has he given? Tell us, Kliwon," Wimpie said, suddenly calm once more. There was an arrogant tone to Wimpie's voice. He wanted the men to know what had been done, especially Pastor who continued sitting calmly in place, his legs now dangling from the *balai*.

"About a half hour's walk from here we'll find a crossing."

"What route are we supposed to take out of here?" Wimpie interrupted.

"Pak Hasan is going to clear a path up to the camp. By tomorrow evening it should be passable."

"In one day? How's that possible?"

"It's possible. There's lots of open places and not that much brush to cut."

"And then?"

"Then, after following the path, we come to a crossing over the old river bed."

"Is there still water?"

"Yes and lots of brush in the bed too. But there's a footbridge made from tree trunks. We spent all afternoon clearing the brush and vines off it."

"And from there Pak Hasan will take us to that village you told me about?"

"Yes."

The Dutch gave him their complete attention. Pastor appeared to be waiting for the opportunity to say something. Now he took the chance.

"Why is Pak Hasan being so good to us, so willing to help

us out of this predicament?" he asked Kliwon in High Malay which he had studied at the seminary.

The men opened their eyes in surprise. They sensed what Pastor was getting at. Wimpie looked unnerved and angry. Kliwon felt cornered. One second ago he had felt relieved not to be a part of the dispute among the men and somewhat proud as well because he was suddenly the center of attention of all these white men. Now he felt that they were playing games with him, that he was only a pawn in a difficult situation.

"The village is where Pak Hasan comes from," Kliwon answered carefully. In fact, he wasn't sure it was true; he himself had come to this conclusion only that afternoon but having said it, he now had to find a convincing continuation for the story.

"He makes a trip to the village every few months and now is the time."

"Who does he go with?" Pastor asked.

"I can't name names but sometimes people from Taratakbuluh go with him and come back with elephant tusks."

"But this time no one else is going along?" Pastor continued his questioning.

"Since the Japanese came hardly anyone goes with him because there's no place to sell the ivory."

"What's the name of the village?"

Kliwon hesitated. "I don't know. When people talk about it they just call it '*hutan*' or the 'jungle.'"

"You are brave men," Pastor said in Dutch. "Exceptionally brave men, willing to venture off to a place you know only by the name of 'jungle.'"

"The jungle is a damn sight better than hell," Wimpie said in Dutch before asking Kliwon in Indonesian: "What about food? And wild animals?"

Kliwon kept his eyes on Pastor when answering Wimpie's questions. "In the jungle you can live off the land and Pak Hasan is a *pawang*; the wild animals will leave us alone." He hoped the Dutch would believe what he was saying.

Van Roscott and his group of friends appeared to sneer at him as they looked at one another. Even Wimpie looked disappointed.

"What if we can't leave tomorrow? Then what?" Wimpie asked.

"Well, I feel . . . ," Kliwon began hesitantly but gained more confidence as he spoke. "Pak Hasan won't want to wait for us too long, and I think if you asked him, he'd tell you we'd be much safer with him than by ourselves."

"How very interesting all this is," Pastor remarked in Dutch. "An extremely well-crafted piece of fiction."

"What the hell do you want anyway, Pastor!" Wimpie snapped at the man in Dutch, trying to vent some of his anger.

"Listen to me," Pastor advised Wimpie in Dutch. "We already agreed that you would run away and I would stay here. I'm only asking these questions because I'm concerned about your own safety; nothing more. Now may I continue?"

Wimpie had no other choice but to acquiesce. "My pleasure," he grumbled.

Kliwon felt miserable. Here he was in the middle of an argument being conducted in a language he didn't even understand but yet was one that involved himself.

"I believe I've heard enough," Pastor declared after a few moments of silence. "I've asked everything I wanted to ask. Supposing that you do leave, I want us to part as friends. I pray for the safety of you all."

Everyone breathed a sigh of relief. No one said anything. Pastor pulled his legs on top of the *balai* and stretched out on his sleeping mat.

"That village in the jungle," Wimpie said, "how many people live there?"

"About a hundred," Kliwon answered.

"Men and women?"

"Yes, men and women."

"Listen to that!" Wimpie cried to his friends in Dutch. "There's only a hundred people there. That would mean about half men and half women. If we all went, we could take over the village. We'd have the women to ourselves. The men could be our servants. How about that for an idea!"

The men in Wimpie's group laughed loudly. The rest only smiled.

Although he didn't understand what was being said, Kliwon felt his confidence returning. Women. That was a subject of endless discussion. At this point, what could be more attractive to them than the thought of a woman? Kliwon felt that this might be the key to freeing himself from Wimpie's hold.

Wimpie's hold was smothering him and the only reason for it was his own stupidity. The story had begun two months earlier in Pakanbaru. In front of the barracks in Rintis, the village where the Dutch prisoners and Japanese soldiers lived, stood a row of food stalls. Similar in size and shape with woven bamboo walls and thatch roofs, the *warung* were operated by local people and served as their homes as well. During his stay in Rintis, Kliwon had come to be on good terms with Siti, the wife of one of the *warung* owners. Siti often complained to Kliwon about her husband and his habit of spending his nights gambling in the *warung* at the end of the row. One night, after most of the stalls were closed, Kliwon called on Siti.

"Any food left?" Kliwon asked Siti as she opened the door.

"Sure, help yourself," the woman told him as she returned to the *balai* to lie back down beside her sleeping children.

"Where is your husband?" Kliwon asked, pretending not to know.

"Where else if not gambling?"

Kliwon didn't take a seat immediately. He walked slowly to the *balai* and positioned himself next to the woman. Siti said nothing.

"When will he be back?" he inquired.

"Not until morning," Siti replied as she stretched out and looked up at Kliwon.

The flickering palm oil lamp was the only witness to the passion that then ensued. No questions asked. No answers given. A simple need fulfilled without the element of emotion. After they were finished, Kliwon put on his clothes and left, just like that.

And the following night. And the night after. Until one night Siti's husband came home earlier than usual and Kliwon became the quarry of all the *warung* owners. His pants in his hands, Kliwon fled through the back door and into the bushes behind the row of *warung*. Gradually, he circled his way back to the barracks.

Beginning the following day Kliwon did not leave the barracks. Whenever he thought about leaving, the sight of four or five men standing beside Siti's *warung* stopped him. About a week later Major Shinji handed him over to Lieutenant Ose at the train station. That is how he came to be in Taratakbuluh.

Of the detainees it was only Wimpie who had been willing to listen to Kliwon when he began to relate his amorous adventure. "You're quite a man, Kliwon, quite a man," Wimpie had said and Kliwon felt extremely pleased with himself. He told his tale again and again until even the smallest of details had been related and magnified beyond life size.

A few days later Wimpie came to him with the warning: "You have to be careful, Kliwon. Taratakbuluh isn't so far from Pakanbaru. If those men should come up here looking for you on a Wednesday when you're off to the market with Freddie, there wouldn't be anything I could do to protect you. They might even kill you."

A few days later: "You have to escape, Kliwon. The work on the embankment is almost finished and soon we'll be sent back to Pakanbaru."

A few days later Kliwon informed Wimpie what he had heard about Paktua Hasan.

One day Wimpie told him: "If you run away, I think I might go along with you." Since that time Kliwon had felt himself tied to Wimpie more tightly by the day. All of the ideas and plans he suggested to Paktua Hasan came from Wimpie and soon the escape that he had originally envisioned was of a completely different form altogether. Yet he didn't have the courage to say no. Wouldn't it be simpler to accept Haji Zen's offer of a place to hide in the village? No, Wimpie wouldn't allow that. A brute like Wimpie might mention something to Lieutenant Ose or send a message to Haji Zen about the real reason for his flight from Pakanbaru.

Now he could see a way to free himself completely from Wimpie. He would go with the other men but they would let themselves be seduced by the women in the jungle village. He would then return to Taratakbuluh with Paktua Hasan where he would accept Haji Zen's offer of a place to hide and, if fate were working for him, marry the man's daughter. Lena was fond of him, wasn't she? Didn't she look at him in the same way that Siti did when they embraced?

"There's a lot of women there," Kliwon said to no one in particular.

❖

When the bell outside sounded four times, signaling that it was four o'clock in the morning Tokyo time, Satiyah awoke. Careful not to make a sound, she stepped out of her doorless bedroom with its woven bamboo walls and went directly to the kitchen. The wooden floor of the hut had not been put together very well and if she didn't watch where she stepped she was sure to set the floor boards creaking. On the short table in the front room the palm oil candle still glowed. Beside it were Lieutenant Ose's dirty dishes. Satiyah tiptoed to the table, picked up the dishes, and carried them back to the kitchen.

Satiyah dished up some rice and a side dish for herself and began to eat. She couldn't recall ever having fasted at her parents' home in Mersi, a village located at the edge of Purwokerto in central Java. It was only later, after her marriage to Ndoro Alimin, a teacher at the Angka Loro School in Mersi, that she had begun to fast and learned how to pray. Nonetheless, during the fasting month and always near its close, even her parents' home was alive with women's activities: the preparation of sweets, *ketupat,* and dishes good to eat with the *ketupat.* For Satiyah, fasting had come to have its own special meaning. It was a ritual she felt she truly understood.

It was a quiet and still night. The sound of the drum from the village across the river had long since faded. Not even the sound of soldiers talking or laughing was audible tonight. All Satiyah could hear was an occasional long and drawn-out sigh from behind the screen where Lieutenant Ose slept. Satiyah sensed that Lieutenant Ose was still awake but she continued to eat and allow her thoughts to wander.

Something must be disturbing Ose, she thought. He probably needed a woman. Even if he didn't, a woman might be able to lighten whatever burden was troubling him. If Ose were to come to her, would she be willing to serve him? She didn't know. Ose was a kind and gentle man, a patient and generous man, in fact very similar to what Satiyah imagined as the perfect man. But he was Japanese and her first experience with a Japanese had been revolting and had almost caused her death.

It had been for that same reason she had run away from Mersi in the first place. She had gone to Jakarta because she heard that other women from her village had been able to find work there as servants. The life of a servant was certainly a step down from her position as the wife of a teacher but what else could she do? Her skills were limited and continuing to live in Mersi was now out of the question. With her mind made up on what she had to do she took her three children to her mother and one night, near dawn, walked out of the village and toward the train station in Purwokerto.

It wasn't until the next morning that the train drew into the Kota Station of Jakarta. Satiyah had watched most of the train's passengers disembark at stations before Kota but she was going to Jakarta and that was the final stop on the route. Earlier the train car had been jampacked with all shapes and sizes of people. Now it was almost empty. Only a few passengers remained and Satiyah relaxed and enjoyed the few minutes of the journey that were left as the train chugged its way slowly toward Kota Station.

After taking care of her bodily needs in the filthy and foul-smelling public bathroom, Satiyah stood confused in front of the station. Where was she to go? Where could she find work as a servant? Around her stood only large buildings and warehouses. Not a single home in sight with a husband, wife, and children. To the left of the station was a row of Chinese shops. Should she try there? She hesitated, unsure. As the sun approached its zenith, Satiyah went to a *warung* to eat.

"I'm looking for work, Pak," she said to the owner of the food stall after finishing her meal.

The man looked at her suspiciously. "As what?" he asked briefly.

"Anything, Pak. I'll even work as a servant."

"If it's a servant you want to be, you shouldn't have come here, Miss. Menteng is where the rich people live," the owner of the *warung* advised.

"Where's Menteng, Pak?"

Other customers in the *warung* began to pay attention to Satiyah.

"Where are you from?" one of them asked.

"Purwokerto," Satiyah answered.

"Are you married?"

"My husband is dead."

"Where are you staying in Jakarta?"

"I don't know. I just arrived this morning," Satiyah answered with unfeigned honesty.

Now everyone paid attention to her. Even though her skin was fairly dark, it showed signs of good care. She was a fairly attractive woman and her clothes were unlike those of most women who were forced to work.

"How would you like to go along with the Japanese to Sumatra?" one of the men inquired.

50

Satiyah didn't know what to say. The thought of working for the Japanese, much less going to Sumatra, had never entered her mind. She didn't know what to answer.

"Everyone is working for the Japanese now. At least with the Japanese you know where your next meal is coming from. That's not true with one of your own. Yeah, better to get a job with the Japanese. You'd only have to take care of one person. You'd live fairly well and have enough money to send some back home." So advised the owner of the *warung*.

It didn't take too much time to convince Satiyah that the best thing for her to do would be to go along with the Japanese to Sumatra. The man who first proposed the plan paid for her meal and ordered her to wait for him to return. A short time later Major Shinji arrived at the *warung*.

The look Major Shinji gave her was one of satisfaction but she found it rude and discomfiting. Nonetheless, that same evening she went to Jakarta's harbor, Tanjungpriok, and boarded the ship that was bound for Sumatra.

Hundreds of Javanese men were on the boat, *romusha* being taken to Sumatra to continue construction on the railroad from Pakanbaru to Sijunjung. In his position on the staff of the Rail Communications Command, Shinji made several trips to Java each year to pick up new *romusha* but all of the *romusha* were men.

That night it happened. Shinji forcibly raped Satiyah. Satiyah yelled and screamed but they were alone in Shinji's cabin and the door was locked. No one could even hear her cries.

"Kangmas Alimin, what kind of curse have you put on me?" Satiyah had screamed when the incident took place but afterward, when it was over, she took the major's bayonet that was lying on the chair and plunged it into her stomach.

The incident put the whole ship in an uproar. The *romusha* screamed and shouted. They had assumed the woman would be raped but that she had been murdered afterward was completely beyond reason. The Japanese soldiers stood at attention, their weapons ready. Some of the officers suggested that the woman be thrown into the sea but the ship's doctor was able to save her.

Satiyah lived with Shinji in the Japanese garrison in the village of Rintis located on the outskirts of Pakanbaru but Shinji never once tried to approach her again. Satiyah kept a *belati*, a small dagger, inside her waistband. Shinji became the laughingstock of the officers in Pakanbaru but he accepted their jokes in good humor. At the very least, he put up with them until a year later when he found the opportunity to present Satiyah to Lieutenant Ose.

Ose was different from Shinji.

After a few days in Taratakbuluh, Satiyah put away the dagger she had kept in her waistband. Ose reminded Satiyah very much of her dead husband, Ndoro Alimin, or as she called him, Kangmas Alimin, a man from a *santri* family who taught at the Angka Loro School in Mersi.

Supposing that Ose came to her now as night was edging toward dawn she would accept him as she would her husband.

Ose remained where he was.

TWO

Momotaro-san, Momotaro-san,
Okoshi ni tsuketa kibidango,
Hitotsu o watashi ni kudasai na.

Peach Boy, Oh Peach Boy,
The cakes that you now carry,
Give me one, please give me one.

Even as the dawn rose on that Wednesday in mid August,
2605, Lieutenant Ose lay awake. He didn't move. He simply
lay there atop his mattress on the floor behind the cloth
screen that separated his sleeping area from the rest of
the room.

He heard Satiyah wake up and listened to her clear away
the short table in the center room and eat her early morning meal before going back to bed again. He listened to her
as she lay in her bed and, like him, unable to sleep, turn
over and then back again on her mat in the small back
room. What was she thinking about? Ose wondered.

During the past few days Ose had sensed that Satiyah
was paying much more attention to him than she normally
did. He was sure that the woman was fond of him just as he
was fond of her. In a faraway country like this she seemed
to be the ideal choice of a woman for him. In fact, if he
wanted her, he knew it wouldn't be difficult. All he would
have to do would be to walk into her bedroom; she would
not refuse him.

53

But no, Satiyah was a religious woman. Ose failed to understand why she would voluntarily endure hunger. She was somewhat of a surprise to him but he felt a good deal of respect for her and thought he knew why she had tried to kill herself after being raped by Shinji.

Here, the situation would be entirely different. If he were to go to her room, no rape would ensue. Their union would be a mingling of two souls long used to suffering and their contact would excite an explosion of affection. Thereafter he would be tied to this woman. At some point, after the end of the war, he would take her home to his motherland where she would become the focus of endless comment. How, in Japan, could this dark-skinned woman be a symbol of love? Impossible. Instead, she would be the butt of scorn, a low woman born from a race without culture or tradition. Weeks would pass before Ose's mother and his two sisters would even venture from their homes because of the shame they would feel and the fear of what the neighbors would say. Ose smiled nervously.

But now was not the time to think about Satiyah and things of a lighter nature. Larger and more frightening questions occupied his mind, questions he could not forget no matter how he might try. The great war that was supposed to have given birth to the Greater East Asian Co-Prosperity Sphere was now coming to an end. How would it end? Why did headquarters say they didn't know?

Because of the spirit of *bushido* instilled in every Japanese soldier, which he himself had gained after his entrance into the Dai Nippon Royal Army, he would not find it surprising to receive orders for *jibaku*. Recognizing their sacred oath, the Japanese people would rise up to defend the motherland and to protect the *Tennō Heika* from attack and shame by the Allied forces. All Japanese—both men and women, young and old, big and small—would surrender their lives for this noble goal. Michiko, his unfaithful wife, his friend Shinji, the priests in the Shinto temples and Buddhist shrines, merchants, civil servants, workers, everyone.

Even his two children. And his simple father as well, a man who bowed to everyone he met during his daily route. And he too. Even those who had never even wanted the war?

For months Michiko and Ose had engaged in a cold war about the real war. Slowly but surely through the late 2590s—the 1930s—the militarists infiltrated all levels of Japanese society. The schools were their first target. During Ose's last year at the Osaka Technical School an instructor was hired to teach the students military theory, a requisite course for all students, one that determined whether they graduated. Every morning before entering class the students had a list of oaths and pledges to recite.

A new instructor joined the staff at the temple where Ose practiced *sumo* twice a week. He instructed the students in new methods of meditation and taught them new oaths and pledges as well. Ose thought of quitting *sumo* but the temple where he studied was that of Priest Ando, the father of Michiko.

Michiko. She was soft and gentle when they first met and while she did indeed laugh at him her patience gave her the ability to instill in him an understanding of the beauty and glory of Japanese traditions. But in the end, she too became infected by the contagious spirit of war.

"Yoshie and Shinji came by earlier. They invited me out to eat," Michiko informed Ose one evening.

"Shinji didn't come into work today," Ose commented.

"I know. He went to the army office to enlist. Yoshie looked so proud."

"They should have thought it over before making such a major decision."

"They did think it over, for a long time, and they've made their resolution for the new century," Michiko informed him, somewhat disappointed by his response.

The year 2600 *Showa* or A.D. 1940 was only a few weeks old. Ose recalled the city's huge celebration on the eve of the new century. It had been a night for resolutions, a night when people made plans for the future and decided what kind of life they wanted. Ose made no decisions that night. He was content with his life, with his beloved wife, and with his work at the construction company in Osaka.

Ose paid little attention to what his wife had said.

A few days later she brought up the subject again.

"All of my friends' husbands have enlisted," Michiko said.

"Darling," Ose said, "we have one child and another on the way. What would happen to them if I were to be killed in battle?"

"Well, what about Yoshie's children? And what about the children of all the other *heitei-san!*" Michiko retorted.

Ose was taken aback. The soft-tempered Michiko he knew was now hard. The lines on her face revealed a rigidity and hardness he had never seen before.

"To keep this country running there must be soldiers, farmers, civil servants, and even construction coolies like myself," Ose said lightly in an attempt to ease the tension.

"But how am I supposed to show my face to my friends whose husbands have gone off to war to defend this country?"

When Ose returned home from work a few days later he found hanging in the center room a banner of white cloth. Written in red *kanji* on the banner was a Kami teaching: "Place the eight corners of the world beneath one roof."

A debate ensued from that night onward. It was only when Ose finally decided to enlist that some kind of peace returned to the house. But the peace was false and one-sided.

"Whatever happens to you, I will be faithful. When you return home I hope it shall be as a hero but if something should happen I promise to take care of our children to the best of my ability." That is what Michiko had told him when they were alone together at a restaurant celebrating his enlistment in the same way that Yoshie and Shinji had done before them.

The Zeni Division from Osaka was first sent to Shanghai and from there transferred to Vietnam. In the summer of 1941 Lieutenant Ose went home on leave. That was the last

56

time he saw Michiko as his wife and should there be a *jibaku*, the last time that he set foot on the soil of his motherland.

It seemed as if there should be another choice.

Japan's industrial cities were destroyed. Hiroshima and Nagasaki had been wiped off the map by secret bombs of the United States. One by one the islands in the Pacific that Japan had conquered were being wrested back by General MacArthur. Of course, the Allies were forced to pay a high price for their victories. At least some of the information in the war communiqués that he received must be correct. From what word reached him he knew that the Allied forces had thrown their entire strength into the caldron of war and should the war continue for a few months longer their strength would be exhausted. Thus it wasn't completely out of bounds to hope that the two sides might some day agree to overcome their differences of opinion at the negotiation table. Peace at last!

How beautiful that would be. No winners, yet all sides saved from the loss of face. Was that an impossibility? The Berlin-Rome-Tokyo Axis no longer existed. Italy was a conquered nation and Germany had surrendered. This left Japan alone to face the whole world! The countries that Japan occupied did little to help. In a way they resembled Kliwon. They were busy with their own affairs and felt much closer to their old masters than their new ones who, Ose had to admit, had brought about a great deal of suffering.

Japan was sure to lose. Maybe she had already surrendered. The telephone call from headquarters had left him with more questions than answers. Headquarters should have been straightforward and admitted that Japan was not capable of continuing the war and would soon surrender.

The bell sounded: eight o'clock Tokyo time. The sunlight crept quietly into the hut. The flickering lamp on the table died. Not long after came the sound of the Dutch detainees rising, leaving the barracks, and going down to the river.

The air felt fresh and cool. The morning birds were singing. A soldier ordered the detainees to line up for roll call. The Dutch fell noisily into place but their voices were soon silenced by the crisp voice of Sergeant Kiguchi, who was in charge of the morning roll. A soldier reported in Japanese. Pastor van Roscott gave his report in Indonesian. Ose smiled to himself; Kiguchi didn't understand Bahasa Indonesia.

The three drums in the bath located behind the hut were being filled. That was the job of two of the detainees each morning. The other detainees left for the work site.

Ose later heard the sound of Satiyah rising and beginning to clean the kitchen.

Finally, he fell asleep.

❖

On Wednesday mornings Ose always rose early to give Satiyah money for the weekly shopping. She had never had to ask him for it. In matters of food, Ose was the perfect man: he was not fussy and made very few demands. A very different man from her husband, Ndoro Alimin, who had to have eggs and vegetables every day and wanted beef, liver, and chicken so many times a week. Milk in the mornings. Cakes with his tea. And on and on. Before the Japanese came to Indonesia the salary of a teacher at the Angka Loro School was more than sufficient to fill all of his demands, but not long after their arrival, the real value of his salary vanished.

Prior to the Japanese occupation, Satiyah was able to set aside part of her husband's monthly wage for her mother and the educational needs of her siblings. Her father worked as a machinist at the Seraju Dal Spoorweg Maatschapij and his wage far from filled the family's needs. With the Japanese the situation turned around 180 degrees and through his work on the railroad, her father was able to supplement his income substantially by taking on odd jobs and handling black market trade.

Satiyah visited home every few days and on these visits her mother never failed to give her something for "Den Guru," "The Teacher." Satiyah's marriage to Ndoro Alimin was a very important event for her family because through him the status of her own family was raised. It wasn't that the position of a teacher was highly respected nor that his wage was so many gulden per month; it was because Alimin came from a *santri* family, a deeply religious family with a strong leaning toward Mecca. Rarely was a *santri* girl permitted to marry a non*santri* man. Exceptions were made if the young man was very religious and enjoyed a good position. Similarly, a *santri* man did not take an "ordinary" woman as his wife unless she were truly something special—beautiful, for instance—and when Satiyah was a young woman she was very attractive. Even now, with her large, round eyes and chocolate-colored skin, traces of her former beauty remained. But the suffering she had endured since that time was apparent as well and together they gave her an appearance of total acquiescence and immeasurable patience.

On this Wednesday in mid August, 2605, Ose didn't rise early to give her shopping money. As silently as possible Satiyah first cleaned her doorless room and then the kitchen. Finished, she waited for the *ndoro tuan*, her former masters, to complete their task of filling the drums in the bathroom behind the hut.

She had never dreamed of seeing the day when a white-skinned large-nosed *ndoro tuan* would carry water for her bath. But that was what was happening now and every other day as well. She had always thought that white men were beings of a higher level, deserving of both fear and respect. Communication with such beings was a risky business for on the one hand it could mean honor and respect but on the other it might just as well mean banishment from one's own people.

When Satiyah was nine or ten years old a young woman from Mersi had been taken as the mistress of a white man from Purwokerto. Surti, the young woman, overnight became a "bad woman" and her parents outcasts. All the villagers talked about them, and human waste, wrapped up in neat packages, was often found outside their home when they awoke in the morning. It was some time before Surti's parents found the courage to show their faces in public once more.

Their lives were made miserable and mothers soon took to warning their daughters about the consequences of following Surti's example. Young women of Satiyah's age were determined not to commit the same error. The shame!

In not too long a time, however, after only a few months, the situation changed completely. The change began when people heard that Surti's father had purchased the large piece of land adjacent to the Angka Loro School that faced the Seraju Dal Spoorweg Maatschapij railyard where Satiyah's father worked. Beginning slowly, the pace at which public opinion changed quickened when Surti's parents began construction of a large house on the land they had purchased.

Prior to construction of the house, Surti's parents held a *selamatan* at which an entire goat was slaughtered and divided. The ceremony was held in the afternoon and quite a few people showed up to observe and take part. Surti came home by carriage from Purwokerto. A few people greeted her and maintained pleasant smiles as they engaged in small talk with her.

The *selamatan* and reception that followed the completion of construction on the new house represented the final turning point of opinion and the final blow to the arrogance and pride of the people of Mersi. A bull was sacrificed to provide food for all the people in the village. A *wayang kulit* performance was held on the large front veranda of the house. Petromax lamps were hung all the way from the house to the end of the road across the railroad tracks. Everyone in the village was invited to the feast and from the looks of it, everyone turned out to enjoy the sound of the *gamelan* that played throughout the evening.

And the way that Surti set the stage for her entrance!

After the completion of prayers of thanksgiving led by Pak Kyai, the *gamelan* began to play again. The meal was ready to be served. At this point Surti arrived with her *ndoro tuan* in a chauffeured open automobile. Sporting a *blangkon* and a gray uniform with burgundy stripes on the sides of his trousers and the cuffs of his jacket, the driver of the car looked exceptionally handsome. With a cream-colored suit, black bow tie, and his hair slicked back and combed neatly into place, the *ndoro tuan* appeared absolutely regal.

Surti was a goddess. With the brilliant light of the Petromax lamps shining on the open car as it came into the front yard, the couple looked especially striking. Surti, in a white lace *kebaya*, sat beside her *ndoro tuan*. Light reflected off the jewels in her hair and the brooch that served as a clasp for her *kebaya*. When the driver opened the car door and Surti stepped out, the eyes of every woman present fell on the Pekalongan batik *kain* that Surti wore. Its motif was one never before seen in Mersi.

No less than the *lurah*, the subdistrict head, stood up to bow. He was followed by the *kyai* and then by everyone else present. Bowing, smiling, and even laughing, the *lurah* advanced to greet Surti and her *ndoro tuan*. Coming up behind were the *kyai* and the other guests.

From her place among the other girls of marriageable age, Satiyah paid close attention to the event unfolding before her. She couldn't quite believe her eyes nor could she stop thinking about it.

Satiyah hadn't married a white man but now there were two of them carrying water for her bath. What had become of Surti's *ndoro tuan*, she wondered. All of a sudden she felt wistful and sad.

The sun grew higher but still Ose didn't awake. Having finished preparing his breakfast, Satiyah bathed and put on her best clothes. She wouldn't wait any longer. There was still money from last week's shopping. Ose always gave her more than enough and never asked her to return what was left.

Satiyah closed the back door behind her and walked around the hut to the open ground in front of the security post. In no time at all she arrived at the edge of the railway embankment where the detainees were working. Today, just as she always did when she went past the Dutch, she felt a mixture of uneasiness and expectation rise up inside her. And sure enough, Wimpie had something to say.

"Hey honey, when do you want to try it again?"

A few of the Dutch laughed loudly at this. Satiyah ignored the comment and continued her journey.

"Come back, I have something for you," Wimpie beckoned.

Satiyah arrived at the top of the trestle and began to cross the planks that had been laid end to end between the rails from one end of the bridge to the other.

Arriving at the other side, Satiyah turned left and went down the embankment. Following the river's edge, she walked upstream. Passing by Haji Zen's home, she finally came to the market where once again she was beset by a sense of unease and expectation. Would there be yet another recurrence of what she had faced on previous market days? Would the men undress her with their eyes and the women stare at her in disgust? And the children, the naked and half-naked children, would they tag after her and scream "Japanese whore?" Would she still have to pay more than everyone else did for her purchases?

On her first Wednesday at the market all of this had happened. She had felt cut to the quick but had tried to keep her head up and pretend that nothing had happened. In the end, her final defense was bridged. She had made so many purchases that she wasn't able to carry the load back to the camp by herself. She was forced to ask for help. She went to the largest *warung*, the end building in the row of shops along the river.

"Would you help me, sir?" she asked Haji Usman, the owner of the *warung*. "Would you find someone to help me take these goods across? I'll pay well," she pleaded.

Haji Usman wasn't sure of what to do. The eyes of everyone in the *warung* were on him, especially those of his wife, his children, his in-laws, and grandchildren. On market day everyone gathered at the shop.

Haji Usman ordered one of his grandsons, Yasin, to help Satiyah. In turn, Satiyah presented Yasin not only with a fairly large tip, but with goods that were hard to come by during the Japanese occupation: white sugar and matches. After that, Yasin was always there to help her on Wednesday mornings. Nonetheless, the jibes and insults continued.

Wednesday of the previous week had been the final day of the month of Sya'ban and the day on which animals were slaughtered in preparation for Ramadan, or Bulan Puasa, the month of fasting. Satiyah felt the day had been created especially for her to take revenge on the people of Taratakbuluh for the pain they had inflicted on her. She wanted her revenge to be a sweet one, similar to the one that Surti had taken on the people of Mersi. But she was not Ose's mistress and where was she to find an open automobile, Petromax lanterns, a bull for slaughter, and a *gamelan* orchestra?

On that Wednesday Satiyah acted very ostentatiously and made many more purchases than she normally would. She also bought special herbs and flowers. These she would use for bathing and for washing her hair. She gave Yasin an extra tip that day and in the evening ordered Kliwon to take food she had prepared to Haji Usman's home: a whole chicken cooked in coconut milk.

Would there be more insults today?

Yasin greeted her and took the two baskets she carried.

"Are you fasting?" the twelve-year-old boy asked her.

"I am. Are you?" Satiyah questioned in return.

"I'm trying," the boy answered, unsure of his resolve. He then said nervously, "My grandfather wants you to stop by before you go home. Grandmother has made something for you to eat when breaking your fast."

❖

After completing *subuh* prayers, Haji Zen found it difficult to fall back to sleep. His mind wandered back and forth. The previous evening he had been convinced that Kliwon's planned departure was a hidden blessing. Now, even though it was only one and a half months since Kliwon's arrival in

63

Taratakbuluh, he recognized that Kliwon had become almost a part of the family.

The men living in the camp across the river had arrived on a Sunday one and a half months ago. The people of Taratakbuluh had wondered at the time why the Japanese were establishing a camp there and then, when the detainees arrived, what they were going to do. Japanese soldiers and Dutch prisoners were no longer an uncommon sight. The villagers had grown used to their presence when the railroad and the trestle were first built. At that time thousands of Dutch detainees and *romusha* were living outside the village and the latter group took no time at all in establishing a bad name for themselves. The Japanese were harsh and the Dutch prisoners were beaten regularly. Some were beaten to death. Those who died were buried beneath the rail embankment or thrown into the river. The Dutch were cowards. There were thousands of Dutch working on the railroad and only a few hundred Japanese. Yet they complacently followed every order the Japanese gave and didn't even raise a hand when struck.

And the *romusha!* What was there to say? The Japanese were lax in their supervision of them and every day, in broad daylight and at night, they would slip into the village to steal anything that could be eaten. They ate things that even the poorest people in the village wouldn't touch: rats, banana trunks, rubber seeds. For the people of Taratakbuluh the word *romusha* soon became a synonym for disgust.

On that Sunday evening six weeks ago a *romusha* had come to his house. It was Kliwon. At the time Haji Zen was repairing his raft at the edge of the river in front of the house. His was the only family in the village that had its own raft for use in bathing, washing clothes, and taking care of other more personal needs. The raft was made of forty bamboo poles laced together in two layers with planks set at intermittent spaces between the two. At the tapered end of the bamboo poles on the downstream side was a small house-like structure that was used as a toilet. The raft was anchored parallel to the river's edge. When the water was high the whole raft was visible from the house but when the water was low one could see only the peak of the outhouse. The raft was usable both in high water and low water.

Haji Zen was on his raft when a young man dressed in oversized Japanese military wear suddenly appeared on the river bank.

"Excuse me, Pak Haji," the young man inquired; that Haji Zen was in fact a *haji* was apparent to everyone because he never took off his pilgrim's hat, even when he was working. "Is there a *warung* nearby?"

Haji Zen looked at the man suspiciously. A Javanese for sure and probably a *romusha*. But his clothes were too good for a *romusha*. He must have stolen them because they were much too large. But who would dare to steal from the Japanese?

"If you're looking for a large *warung*, there isn't one," Haji Zen finally replied. "But there's a small one if it's daily supplies you want. Over that way," Haji Zen said as he pointed in the direction of Haji Usman's *warung*. "The dark two-storied one."

"Thank you," the young man said and went on his way.

Haji Zen watched him walk away. He carried himself well and seemed friendly. Maybe he was an employee of the Japanese and not a real *romusha*.

A little while later the young man passed by again, this time with a parcel in his hand. He stopped and came down the bank.

"I found it," he said while placing the package on the ground.

"Get everything you need?" Haji Zen asked him just to have something to say.

"Wasn't much I needed. Just some dried fish, salt, and chilies. Aren't there any vegetables around here?" he asked.

"On Wednesdays there are," Haji Zen answered. "Are you living here?" he then asked.

"I live at the camp across the river. I'm a *romusha*. My name is Kliwon."

So, a *romusha* after all, Haji Zen thought, but one who little resembled his former image of *romusha*. This one was clean, polite, and friendly.

Kliwon boarded the raft and began to help Haji Zen tighten the wire bindings that held the bamboo poles together.

"What's your job over there?"

"I'm not even sure myself, Pak Haji. I'll probably help the cook. Maybe something else. I've not been told. In Pakan-baru I carried water for the Japanese army barracks."

"Where are you from originally?"

"Pacitan, sir, in Java."

"What did you do there?"

"I worked in the office of the *kelurahan*. I was in charge of recruiting *romusha*."

"If you were in charge of recruiting *romusha* then what are you doing here?

"The people there got angry with me. They said their boys had been taken away and sent to who knows where. There hadn't been any word from those who had gone and since none of them had returned no one was sure whether they were alive or dead. They 'suggested' that I go and so I thought maybe I should. I led one of the groups from my village, the third group."

For a while neither of the two men spoke as they worked.

"Some of them are dead now. Others, I don't know what's happened to them," Kliwon finally added.

Haji Zen invited Kliwon to the house for tea.

On Wednesday, market day, Kliwon complained to Haji Zen of the difficulty of finding vegetables in Taratakbuluh.

"There's so much land around here. Why don't people plant their own vegetables?" Kliwon asked.

"I don't know. I guess no one has ever tried."

"What if I try planting some in that brushy area behind the house?" Kliwon suggested.

66

No harm in trying, Haji Zen concluded. Why hadn't he thought of it before?

"Sure, Kliwon. If you want to try to raise a garden, go right ahead."

Kliwon came back that same evening to cut away the scrub brush behind the house. He ate with the family that night and, more significantly, accompanied them in their prayers.

The garden was fairly large and coming along successfully. Some of the plants were already a span high. Kliwon came by every evening to see if anything had to be done: watering, weeding, or setting out new plants.

Kliwon was like a member of the family. So why was he helping him run away? If something were to happen to Kliwon . . . No, Hasan was a reliable man. But if there were an accident?

At about eight o'clock that morning Haji Zen set off for the market. It was still quiet; boats from villages along the Kampar Kanan that were close to Taratakbuluh had just begun to arrive. Vendors were arranging their goods on mats they had stretched out on the ground. The Minang peddlers stood by the river approaching each of the boats as they arrived, hoping to buy wholesale anything they might be able to sell in Pakanbaru.

Haji Zen went directly to Haji Usman's *warung* where he found Hasan already waiting for him. Hasan rose at once but Haji Zen motioned for him to sit.

"Buy some new *parang*, about ten of them," Haji Zen said to Hasan as he handed him a sum of money. "Use the rest of the money to buy the other things you'll need."

Hasan took the money and counted it. A tidy sum, he thought, but Haji Zen could well afford it. He owned at least five fish traps—or was it seven—and half the boats in the village. He also owned houses and quite a number of shops.

After Hasan left, Haji Usman sat down on the newly vacant chair.

"*Assalamu'alaikum,*" Haji Usman said in greeting to Haji Zen.

Haji Zen turned toward him. "*Wa' alaikum salam,*" he answered immediately. "I think we've got this backward. You are the host after all. I should have greeted you first."

"Don't worry about it," Haji Usman laughed. "Maybe I am the host but I can't offer you anything to drink."

"Wouldn't matter if you did," Haji Zen joked in return. "I wouldn't drink it anyway!"

The two men laughed. Haji Usman, a fairly small man, noted how large Haji Zen seemed in comparison. His mind searched rapidly for a way to begin the conversation he had planned.

"Is Kliwon planning to escape?" he suddenly asked Haji Zen.

Haji Zen stopped laughing and looked at Haji Usman. Hasan must have said something, he thought. But there was no need to keep secrets from Haji Usman.

"It looks like it," Haji Zen answered.

"He's a good lad," Haji Usman commented.

"Good or bad is yet to be seen. He has been here for only a month and a half now. If he wants to escape, that's his choice but, because he's treated me well, I'll treat him even better."

Haji Usman fell silent. He knew that his conversational abilities were no match for those of Haji Zen. Haji Zen always had something to say in any kind of situation. Haji Usman searched for an opening line, some way to direct the conversation. His own daughters were married and when representatives of the families of their future husbands had asked for their hands in marriage he had seen no one at a loss for words. They knew exactly what to say. Which one of them had said: "Our child is grown, a bird ready to try its wings. If his wings should carry him here he might help you mend the broken stairway or carry your clothes to the river to be washed"? He couldn't remember, but he did know that Harun, his brother-in-law, had been able to respond accordingly. Likewise, when his son was to marry,

Harun was the one who had represented the male side in delivering the proposal.

Haji Zen sensed that Haji Usman wanted to talk to him about something. For that reason, he made no move to leave and concentrated his attention on the market that was now coming to life. More and more boats were arriving. The vendors had almost finished putting their goods on display. The Minang peddlers were making purchases and stacking the goods they bought near the items they intended to sell. Barely dressed children gathered according to age and gender and began to play and scream. Vendors who were still trying to arrange their wares kept having to chase the children away from the selling locations they had claimed.

The sun peeked over the tops of the rubber trees behind the railroad. People from other settlements nearby began to arrive by foot and by boat.

"I have been asked to make a request of you, Pak Haji," Haji Usman began nervously.

Haji Zen turned to face Haji Usman. His friend spoke as if he were afraid of something, as if he had been caught doing something wrong.

"Then you must honor that request." Haji Zen smiled and maintained a pleasant tone.

"Anis, the young man you met last night . . ."

That's it, thought Haji Zen. Why hadn't he thought of the possibility before?

". . . asked me if it might be possible to visit you some time." Haji Usman felt he now had enough courage to continue the conversation.

"I have no objections," Haji Zen answered. "Do you mean today?"

"Tomorrow," Haji Usman answered briefly.

"But doesn't he go back to Pakanbaru today?"

"Yes, but he would come back here again tomorrow."

This is fast, Haji Zen thought. Obviously, Kliwon's planned departure had some influence on the choice of time. But what did that matter anyway? If a decision were to be made it would be his and Lena's to make.

"Doesn't this seem a little hasty? Would this have anything to do with Kliwon's departure?" Haji Zen asked.

"No, not at all," Haji Usman answered nervously. "Last night, before *tarawih*, Anis told me what he wanted me to do. So I thought I'd take care of his request right away. Better than putting it off."

"Whether Kliwon is here or not, I see no problem in Anis coming to visit. The choice is up to him. If he wants to visit today, fine. If he wants to visit tomorrow, that is fine too. Did he happen to say anything else?"

"Well, he did say that he's completely alone here with no friends or family, which is why he has put his trust in me."

"He's not married, is he?" Haji Zen inquired.

Haji Usman didn't know what to say. He hadn't thought about that possibility.

"I've not asked him, Pak Haji. But, I don't think so," he answered slowly.

Haji Zen realized that it was beyond Haji Usman's capabilities to find out that kind of information. He had his own way of finding information; by asking a question point blank and watching the face of the person he was speaking to, he could find out all he needed to know.

"All right, then," Haji Zen proposed. "Why don't you come to the house tomorrow before *magrib*. We can break fast together."

After chatting for a few moments longer, Haji Usman left Haji Zen to tend to his business in the store. Meanwhile, the morning train from Pakanbaru pulled into Taratakbuluh, then left. A half hour later the morning train from Sijunjung to Pakanbaru arrived. People who were assigned to take care of Haji Zen's business affairs came to the *warung* to settle their accounts with him and wait for additional orders.

The sun rose higher. At about twelve o'clock Hasan returned to the *warung* with a few bundles of goods. After leaving a message for Kliwon, he walked down to the river, stepped into a *perahu*, and began to row upstream.

70

❁

The first important thing to happen that Wednesday morning was the announcement made by Freddie the cook shortly after the men awoke. "I'm going with you, Wimpie," he said.

The men in Wimpie's group laughed loudly. Pastor and his group looked crestfallen. The men in Freddie's group, the in-between group, looked confused. Now they would be forced to make a choice, something that none of them had wanted to do. Wimpie was elated by this new turn of events but tried not to show delight.

Freddie's group was the largest, fourteen men in all, and in the end most of them decided to join in the breakout. Together with Wimpie's group, this made twenty men planning to run away. Those who wished to stay were, in general, the older ones. They now sat alone, lost in thought.

On Wednesdays the men usually ate their midday meal earlier, at about one thirty Tokyo time. Following the meal, Freddie and Kliwon would make their way across the bridge and to the market. At that time of the day business at the market was beginning to die and they were able to buy what remained of the morning sale of food at a relatively low price. This helped them stretch the pittance they were granted as a food allowance.

That day the men bought a week's supply of food for only ten people, the number expected to remain behind. They spent the rest of the money on supplies they would need in the jungle: salt, a few knives (the Japanese were sure to smell something if they purchased *parang*), rope, flint, flintstones, and tinder (no matches were available). They also bought cakes of red palm sugar (white sugar was not to be had), quinine tablets whose coating had long since dissolved, and a few bottles of what one of the vendors called "all-purpose oil." The oil vendor showed the men his arms, snake-bitten and scarred by broken pieces of glass. It was the oil, the man insisted, that had saved him. The oil was good for almost everything, from knife wounds, animal bites, and sore bones on up to colds and nausea.

71

After making their purchases the men went to Haji Usman's *warung*. Freddie waited there while Kliwon went to Haji Zen's. The Dutchman felt annoyed. Because of the fasting month, he couldn't have his usual cup of coffee. The owner of the *warung* wouldn't sell it. Even so, this brief respite from the camp was a pleasant interlude for him. Children gathered around and stared at him the way they might at a traveling medicine man.

Freddie had been responsible for the shopping in Pakanbaru too. But there, he was always accompanied by Japanese soldiers and he never once had an opportunity to enjoy a cup of coffee alone or play games with children as he did in Taratakbuluh.

The Japanese soldiers also came to the Wednesday market to shop. They took turns and two were now visible in the middle of the dying market. Leaving the market, they approached Haji Usman's *warung*.

"Drink?" they asked simply.

"Nothing to drink, Masta," Freddie answered straight away.

"Fasting, no sell drink."

Haji Usman was extremely relieved to see the Japanese soldiers go. He didn't know what he would have done had the Japanese insisted that he prepare coffee for them. Everyone would have criticized him for selling food during the daylight hours of fasting month.

Kliwon went into the mosque. People had finished their *lohor* prayers some time ago but Kliwon went to the back entrance and out of the mosque to cleanse himself. Returning, his eyes met those of Haji Zen. The two said nothing and Kliwon prayed by himself in the near empty mosque.

After prayers, Kliwon approached Haji Zen. The two sat together in the back portico.

"Hasan has left," Haji Zen said.

"Did he leave a message for me, Pak Haji?"

"Yes, he did. He said that he has cleared away the brush and that there is now a footpath leading to the camp. It ends only a few feet from the stunted rubber tree behind the barracks."

"But what if there's more than one stunted tree?"

"Hasan said there's only one. That's what you have to look for."

"When did he clear the path? He did that awfully fast, didn't he?" Kliwon asked, somewhat surprised.

"I should have told you long ago," Haji Zen said slowly, "never to doubt Hasan's word. If he says there's a path, believe him; there is a path there."

After a few moments of silence, Haji Zen continued. "If you do run away tonight, do whatever Hasan tells you to do. Never disobey him. I feel that Hasan is somewhat different from the rest of us but he is a good and honest man and will do nothing to bring harm to others. If it were anyone other than Hasan, I would have tried to dissuade you from running away a long time ago."

The two men sat in thought.

At irregular intervals other villagers came to the mosque for *lohor* prayers. Entering from the side portico they went directly to the back portico and outside to cleanse themselves. Coming back, they greeted the two men and went into the central prayer space. After prayers they exited the mosque through the side portico.

"I thought the same thing," Kliwon affirmed.

"Some people have gone with Hasan to the village," Haji Zen began again.

"But none have ever returned," Kliwon replied.

"That's right, but where did you hear that?"

"Oh, people talk, and from Pak Hasan himself. Do you think they were killed?"

"No, I don't," Haji Zen answered with certainty. "They might not have returned to Taratakbuluh but they have come close. Rattan gatherers have seen them and spoken with them. They said they looked fine and in good health but did not want to return."

"Pak Hasan told me that yesterday," Kliwon confirmed.

"Just remember. Do what Pak Hasan tells you to do, especially when you're in the jungle. If you have any intention of returning to the outside world you must strengthen your faith. Life there is supposed to be extremely free. If you should take a woman there you will become one of them and never return."

"I know, sir."

"Don't forget to put your trust in Allah. Be strong."

"I will, Pak Haji."

"I pray to Allah the most powerful that He will provide all of you His protection."

"That is my prayer too, Pak Haji. So then, we are to go through the brush near the stunted tree behind the barracks, is that right?" Kliwon asked.

"Yes, that's what Hasan said. Just a few feet away from the tree you'll find the beginning of the footpath that he cleared."

"Thank you, Pak Haji," Kliwon said again. "If all goes well, we'll leave tonight. I ask for your prayers, Pak Haji, and your blessings and your forgiveness for any wrong I may have committed. When things are back to normal I will return and come directly to your house because, Pak Haji, you have become like a father to me."

Kliwon put his palms together, then bowed his head and kissed the hands of Haji Zen.

Haji Zen felt moved by Kliwon's show of respect. He then said to Kliwon, "Before you go, stop by at the house. I believe Lena and her mother have prepared something for you to take along."

Kliwon returned to Haji Usman's *warung* where he shook hands with the owner.

"I've heard you are going to leave," Haji Usman said in a half-questioning manner.

Kliwon was surprised.

"Don't worry," Haji Usman said to ease Kliwon's suspicions. "All of us pray that you will return safely."

"Thank you, Pak Haji," Kliwon answered.

"I know how difficult it is to work with the Japanese," Haji Usman commented. "One mistake and that could be the end of all of us. Once, there was a *romusha* a day dying around here, sometimes as many as three. So, I say, if you have the opportunity to escape, take it, Kliwon."

"Thank you, Pak Haji."

The two men shook hands again and then Kliwon went over to Freddie who had been silently watching their discussion.

When they were passing by Haji Zen's house, Kliwon asked Freddie to wait for him a moment. Haji Deramah stood expectantly at the door.

"Come in for a bit," she said to Kliwon. Kliwon went into the house while Freddie went down to the raft where he sat leaning against the woven bamboo wall on the raft's river side.

"We have some spiced fish for you. Lena made them herself."

"Thank you. I wish I could stay here and talk but I have to take the food we bought back to the camp and finish making arrangements for our escape tonight."

Lena entered the room carrying with her a small bundle and a *parang* with a carved sheath. Kliwon's heart beat faster as he looked at the girl.

Lena's face reminded him of a sudden afternoon rain that can turn the body hot, then cold. She looked wistful yet strong at the same time. She seemed to have something on her mind as she smiled and looked at him with her round, clear eyes.

"Here's a sarong and a *parang* for you to take along. You might need them," she said.

It was forbidden to take weapons into the camp but the Japanese had never searched him before. He could hide the *parang* in the basket of food.

"Thank you, Lena," Kliwon said. He was now sure that Lena cared for him and did not want to see him go.

"You won't forget us, will you?" Lena asked with forced laughter.

"I won't," Kliwon answered, feeling somewhat abashed and confused.

Haji Deramah went to the kitchen and came back with a parcel.

"This is the fish that Lena made," she said as she gave him the bundle.

Kliwon felt the world growing absolutely still. Is this

then the real meaning of parting? he asked himself. When he said good-bye to his parents in Pacitan, his home village, he had been in high spirits, confident of his dreams of prosperity for Greater East Asia. When he left Pakanbaru it had been with relief from the fear of Siti's husband. Now, leaving Taratakbuluh, he felt as if he were leaving behind a part of his soul as well as all his dreams and aspirations for a pleasing and worthy life. How was he to release himself from a dream that was almost sure to become reality?

"I must leave, Bu Haji, Lena," he said, trying to suppress his feelings. "I ask you for your blessing, prayers for my safety, and forgiveness for any wrong I may have committed."

"Good-bye, Kliwon," Lena answered, a faint smile on her lips. The look of an afternoon rain remained on her features.

"Be careful, Kliwon, and keep your trust in God," Haji Deramah advised. "When things have calmed down, come back."

❧

Ose didn't awake until midday. He now felt somewhat refreshed and free from the confusion that had plagued his thoughts the night before. He pulled aside the curtain that separated his sleeping area from the rest of the room. Standing quickly he took his towel and went out to the back to bathe. Satiyah was preparing lunch for him in the kitchen but he did not greet her. They rarely spoke if it were not necessary.

Coming back from his bath, Ose found that Satiyah had already placed his meal on the short table in the center room. He put on official dress and sat down crosslegged at the table to eat. It was then he remembered something.

"Satiyah-san," he called.

Satiyah came to him.

"I forgot to give you money for the market," Ose said while taking money from his trouser pocket.

"Don't worry, Masta," Satiyah assured him, "there was still some money from other shopping trips."

"Here, take it anyway," Ose said as he gave her a wad of money.

Satiyah accepted the money without remark.

"I will be going to Pakanbaru," Ose informed her. "Please pack my clothes," he said.

Satiyah looked as if she wanted to say something but she didn't.

"I'll be back tomorrow," Ose added.

Without replying, Satiyah fetched the knapsack Ose usually used for his clothing and personal effects when going to Pakanbaru.

"Have you eaten?" Ose inquired of Satiyah.

"No, Masta. I'm fasting."

"That's right. I forgot."

Silence again. The two went on with their individual activities: Ose eating and Satiyah readying Ose's clothing. Whenever Satiyah packed Ose's knapsack she thought of her husband, Ndoro Alimin, the respected *santri*. Four months after the Japanese took control in Indonesia, the orders had come for the younger school teachers to attend a crash course in Japanese. Ndoro Alimin was chosen to represent the Angka Loro School.

A bright future lay ahead. Alimin would soon become an important teacher at the Angka Loro School, possibly more important than Ndoro Siman, the school's principal. Ndoro Siman was getting on in years, wasn't he? It would be extremely difficult for him to study something entirely new. Wasn't he almost due to retire? What greater happiness could she hope for than to be the wife of the school principal?

No matter what sacrifices were required for the realization of that goal, she would make them. She was pregnant with her third child and Lebaran, the day ending the fasting month, was only two and a half months away, but Ndoro Alimin was required to reside at the dormitory in Semarang for three months. Surely he would have some vacation, wouldn't he? As a sign of his determination to succeed, Ndoro Alimin shaved off his thick wavy hair a few days before he was to leave.

Satiyah made fun of her husband when she was collecting the clothes that he was to take with him: "Your *pici* is going to be too big for you, Mas," she laughed loudly.

"That's all right," her husband answered. "I'll buy a new one; one that fits just right."

"You better take your old one anyway, Mas."

"There's no need to do that."

"There is too! For sleeping! Your poor little head is going to be cold."

Realizing that Satiyah was making fun of him, Alimin grabbed a ruler and chased his wife around the room.

Satiyah laughed and held her large stomach. "No, Mas, be careful. The baby . . ."

"All right, give me your hands. I'm going to rap your knuckles ten times." He tried speaking to Satiyah as he would to a student but could not keep from laughing.

"But my hands didn't do anything wrong, Mas," Satiyah pleaded.

"What did then?"

"My mouth."

"Okay, give me your mouth."

They kissed. Later that night they expressed their affection for each other once more with passionate, yet careful lovemaking. "Be careful, Mas. The baby," Satiyah was forced to remind her husband time and again.

The sexual needs of Satiyah's husband, the man who had become the pride of her family and who had once been the most sought-after young man in Mersi, were voracious. They made love at least once a night. Satiyah served her husband willingly and with happiness and pride.

"Will you come home when the baby is born?" Satiyah asked her husband before he left.

"Of course I will."

"And for Lebaran?"

"There should be a three-day vacation."

It had never occurred to Satiyah that her husband might not be able to come home for their third child's birth or for Lebaran either. It was even less imaginable that when her husband did finally come home, after the end of the course

78

in late October, he would no longer be her husband in the true sense of the word. But that is what happened. Gone was all the warmth and passion she once shared with her husband. Gone were the nights of pleasure and pride.

After finishing his meal, Ose went to the security post where he found only Kiguchi and another soldier.

"I am going to Pakanbaru," he informed Kiguchi. "Please prepare the necessary papers for transfer of authority."

"*Hai!*" Kiguchi said in compliance.

Kiguchi took the log, filled in the agenda just as he always did when Ose went away, and then signed it. Ose then affixed his signature to the log.

"Have Kliwon come by at 1800 hours to pick up my bag."

"*Hai!*"

Sergeant Kiguchi was 100 percent military. A simple man, Ose thought. The most often heard expression from his mouth was *hai*, or "yes, sir," and that statement alone was enough to reveal what the man was thinking. The previous night, for instance, Ose had sensed that Kiguchi wanted to conceal his observations on the recent behavior of the Dutch detainees and then later, as he often did, do what he thought was best to settle the problem. Ose was sure that Kiguchi would do something while he was away and, in that, knew there was little that he could do to stop him.

For Kiguchi, war was like a game that children played. One group of children stayed inside the fort they had built to defend themselves against the other group. Later the two groups changed positions but, even as the battle raged, there was still time enough to break fences, steal and devour fruit from the neighbor's garden, stone the cats and dogs, and make girls scream by whipping their dolls and throwing them in the gutter. What excitement!

"I think the war is almost over," Ose said to Kiguchi.

"*So deska!* Is that right?" Kiguchi replied in a monotone.

Kiguchi's face showed no emotion. The War God up above had been sufficiently generous to grant him a wide enough variety of experiences to have made this war an enjoyable one: he had killed enemy soldiers and tried the women of different countries. His series of adventures would provide him an unending source of conversation in the days ahead and a wellspring of spiritual satisfaction from which to draw nourishment for the rest of his life.

Ose would have liked to hear Kiguchi's opinion about the outcome of this war but he refrained from asking him. Rarely were people like Kiguchi capable of interesting or incisive comment.

"Try to make sure that everything goes well. Keep things in order," Ose advised.

"*Hai!*"

It had taken hardly any time at all for the Dai Nippon Army to shake the world and to conquer the best divisions of countries formerly considered the strongest and most advanced in the world. The Japanese army had taken over most of the Asian continent and the Pacific, an area that had once been thought impregnable. What had been thrown into battle to assure victory? Hundreds and thousands of soldiers like Kiguchi. The man's stupid and simple-minded appearance appalled him.

"Don't do anything excessive," Ose told Kiguchi.

"*Hai!*"

Ose knew that his orders would not be followed. This had been proven time and again. Ose was relieved about one thing, however; Kiguchi did his best to keep his actions from leaving a visible sign. That was a mark of progress compared to what went on in other units in which Kiguchi had served. The number of victims that fell under other commanders was staggering. This, at the very least, had not happened in Taratakbuluh.

Ose stood up, intending to return to his hut. Smiling, bowing his head slightly, he patted Kiguchi on the back.

Kiguchi screamed out the orders "Attention!" and "Salute!" which were followed immediately by the one and only other soldier in the post.

Ose shook his head. He felt extremely sad.

Even while tending to his trade that Wednesday morning in mid August, 2605, Anis kept his eyes on Haji Usman's *warung*. Not one thing went by unobserved. After the market closed, the Minang traders returned to Haji Usman's for *lohor* prayers. Then after settling their accounts with the owner of the *warung*, they piled their purchases beside that section of the railway they called "the station." There was no building there, not even a hut. The tradesmen merely piled their goods next to the rail on top of the embankment and then waited for the train beneath the shade of the rubber trees at the embankment's base. Anyone else who wanted a free ride on the coal train had only to follow the example of the Minang traders. As the train came into Taratakbuluh it slowed down enough to allow those who were waiting at the "station" to board, free of charge.

It was only five o'clock Tokyo time. At the earliest, the next train would arrive at six o'clock, after the last train out of Pakanbaru had arrived and left for Sijunjung. The people waiting for the train dozed or engaged themselves in small conversation, anything to keep their minds off their hunger. Some of the traders played dominoes. Anis returned to Haji Usman's *warung*. "You must come back tomorrow," Haji Usman said to Anis immediately. "We have been invited to break fast at Haji Zen's home."

"What do you think my chances are, Pak Haji?"

"I couldn't say," Haji Usman answered. "The customs here might be different from those of your village."

"That's what I wanted to ask you about."

"Here, the prospective groom doesn't usually take part in the proposal ceremony. But in your case, you'll be along so I'm not sure what custom to follow. Even so, I don't think it's very important. Haji Zen himself isn't much of a person for custom. He himself told me to invite you. That should mean you have a fairly good chance."

"What about the *romusha?*"

"He's supposed to be running away tonight."

It wasn't until after seven o'clock that the train to Pakanbaru arrived in Taratakbuluh. Anis took note of Kliwon who was carrying Lieutenant Ose's bag. Lieutenant Ose quickly joined the other Japanese commanders already on the train. The train didn't stop long, only long enough for everyone to board.

As the train slowly made its way toward Pakanbaru, the Minang traders began to sense that something was wrong. Wherever they looked there seemed to be something missing, but it wasn't until the train finally stopped at Simpang Empat Rengkok, the intersection where the road out of Pakanbaru crossed the rail and the point where they got off, that they realized what was missing: the Dutch internees. Throughout the journey they had seen not a single Dutch internee. There were none working, none standing around, none walking to the barracks.

There was no station at Simpang Empat Rengkok but that was where the Minang traders and other passengers on the train usually got off. From that point to Pakanbaru the road was asphalt, and it led through the town's main residential area. Another advantage to disembarking at the crossroads was that it was fairly close to the Batu Satu Market, a new market where the traders were able to stay overnight and store their goods. On both sides of the highway were barracks for the Dutch prisoners of war. Usually at sunset they could be seen lining up, preparing to go back to their barracks, singing in low voices or sometimes just yelling to hear their own voices. Usually there were others on the road being herded back toward one of the camps by Japanese soldiers.

Tonight the area was empty and absolutely quiet. The only people that were visible were a few stone-like Japanese soldiers standing outside the guardhouses located in front of the barracks. Not even residents of the town were about. Possibly that was because it was almost time to break fast. But why weren't there any food vendors out in search of customers?

The Minang traders stood in apparent confusion beside their goods. They looked around with suspicion and caution. Their kind of life was a risky one and a *babelok*, if he were to survive, had to be extremely sensitive to his surroundings and be able to adapt quickly to any change in climate. The ability of a *babelok* to adjust to change determined whether his business prospered or died. A *babelok* was always far ahead of the common man in detecting change. He had to be. He had to have a sixth sense. If a *babelok* were able to predict change and take advantage of it he could become a rich man. If he couldn't he would be one of the fish that line the shore after a sudden rise and drop of the sea.

"The Dutch stopped working at midday," Yassin, the railroad worker who manned the gate at the crossing, informed them. Yassin was originally from Singapore—that was apparent in his accent—and had been a friend of the traders for some time. He was always there to help them load or unload their goods, to find a coolie to cart their goods away, or merely to accompany them in conversation as they waited for the train. The men always brought him something as a kind of payment for his assistance.

"I don't know what's happening around here," Yassin answered. "Around noontime the Dutch were rounded up and taken back to the camp. There's been neither hide nor hair of them since."

The Mangun family home was the only house within a kilometer from the railway-highway crossing. Surrounded by a barbed wire fence, the rest of the area was presently being used as a camp for the Dutch internees. Now all that was visible were the stark barracks, the soldiers' quarters, and a security post beside the entrance to the camp. The Mangun home stood on the same side of the railway as the small guardhouse where Yassin lived and worked. The Mangun home was a large one with an extensive front yard. To the left, right, and back of the home was a multilayered barbed wire fence that had been erected by the Japanese to set off the house from the camp grounds.

The Minang traders enjoyed a friendly, easy-going relationship with Pak Mangun, a retired police officer, and his wife. The Manguns were long past middle age, and their only child was now married and had children of his own. On their trips to and from Pakanbaru the Minang traders stayed with the Manguns. The traders were now the old couple's children, and they never failed to inquire about their needs and bring them something from their travels.

It was to the Mangun home that the traders headed that evening. Mrs. Mangun had already prepared food for them to break fast. The elderly woman appeared nervous and upon their arrival ordered the young men to come quickly into the house. This was not an easy order to carry out because they had to return to Yassin's hut a few times to pick up all their goods. Nonetheless, Mrs. Mangun waited patiently beside the door and each time the men came in with a load of wares she would shut the door quickly again.

"Hurry up, boys," she pleaded with them in a half whisper. "Heaven knows what's happening and here you are taking your time!"

The men laughed, "Don't worry, everything is calm now. There's nothing to be afraid of."

"If I hadn't been waiting for you, I would have gone to Kadar's house this afternoon," the old woman answered.

"But if you went to your son's home, what would have happened to your children here?" one of the men asked while laughing.

The woman blushed and then smiled with pride.

Mr. Mangun had said nothing to them since their arrival but now began to speak. "She told me we should go to Kadar's house. But I said Kadar's house is too small. What with all the children, where would we sleep? Besides, this is our home, bought and paid for with good and honest money we saved for years so that we'd have a place to live in our old age. So, whether we live or die, it's going to be here."

The men took turns bathing and upon hearing the sound of the drum, the sign of *magrib*, they broke fast with a bowl of *kolak*, a sweetened cassava stew that Mrs. Mangun had prepared. Yassin, who had never once in his life fasted but who had helped the traders carry their goods to the Mangun home that night, received a portion too.

After *magrib* prayers and a simple meal the traders discussed what to do. They decided that six men would walk to Batu Satu Market while the rest stayed behind at the Mangun home. The old couple protested vigorously.

"No one is leaving this house. You're all staying here."

The men laughed.

"If anything were to happen to you on the road there wouldn't be anyone to help. No one would even know."

"But if there's no one on the road, then what could possibly happen?" the men laughed in return.

In the end, six of the men set off toward Batu Satu, each with a lighted torch in his hand. Anis was in the group that left. The seven-day moon in the western sky provided enough light to brighten the quiet and empty highway. The men kept their torches burning only to calm the suspicions of homeowners who no doubt were peering at them from behind the closed shutters of their homes.

In front of each of the barracks they passed was a Japanese soldier standing stiffly erect, and whose only sign of life was a slight turn of his head, eyes gazing at them, as they passed. Not too far away they could see the security post where a few more soldiers, three at most, were visible. It wasn't late but there was no sign of life at all in the barracks. Except for the occasional night sound and the hum of the diesel generator that provided electricity for the camp, the night was silent.

In a *langgar,* the small prayer house that stood beside the road, people were engaged in *tarawih* prayers beneath the light of palm oil lamps. As the men moved along the highway, the clear and mournful voice of the prayer leader seemed to follow them. The sound of the diesel generator grew dim. The voice of the *imam* singing verses from the Quran, the sounds of the night, the half moon in the western sky, a rush of cool air—the men felt as if they were in another world. None of the men spoke; no one dared try to shake off the burden of unease that nestled on everyone's shoulders.

The tension the traders felt began to ease only upon their arrival at the Batu Satu Market. No customers were around but the food stalls were still open. This alone was enough to make the men feel as if they had waked from a long and frightening dream. There they parted and went to their respective lodgings.

Agus and his wife, Mar, were surprised to see Anis appear at their door.

"What was it like on the road?" they asked almost in unison.

"Quiet," Anis answered as he entered the house. "What happened anyway?"

"I don't know," Agus replied as he sat down on the mat on the floor. The room in which they sat was a working space during the day. At night, the sewing machine, the family's means of a livelihood, was pushed to the side and the room changed into a sitting area. When Anis stayed overnight, the room was his bedroom as well.

"But it looks like the war is over," Agus added.

Anis was startled by this news and stared at Agus in disbelief.

"Have you eaten?" Mar inquired.

"Yes," he answered her but then turned to Agus again. "What do you mean, 'over'?"

"Just that it might be over. But no one knows for sure."

"Who told you?"

"Everyone's been saying it but no one seems to know what happened. Some say peace, some say America surrendered, others say that Japan surrendered. Let me tell you, a half a day of rumors has been exhausting."

"We didn't get any work done this evening," Mar added.

The men were silent. Mar went into the kitchen and returned with two cups of coffee and what little remained of their meal from breaking fast.

Anis took a deep breath and began to speak slowly. "This could upset all of my plans."

Agus said nothing. He kept his eyes on Anis as he rolled

himself a palm leaf cigarette and lit it on the palm oil lamp that was on the floor beside him.

"I was going to ask you to go with me to Taratakbuluh tomorrow," Anis added upon seeing no response from Agus.

"What is happening in Taratakbuluh?"

"I want to propose to a girl there, the daughter of a *haji*."

"Is she one of our people?"

"No, she's not one of 'our' people. She's from Taratakbuluh. She was born and raised there."

Agus frowned, not ready to offer comment. He sipped the coffee his wife had brought him and gestured for Anis to eat.

Why did this have to happen? Agus was thinking. Anis, being a younger man than he, was his responsibility. That was one of the unwritten rules of the game. As for Anis, a *perantau*, a young man off in search of his fortune, it was his responsibility to return home with the fortune he made and marry a girl from his own village. Such a marriage marked a successful end of a young man's adventures and provided assurance that his village, if it were poor or its land infertile, would have someone to give it life. The Minangkabau people were matrilineal. Property and wealth passed through the woman's side, but if young men chose not to return from their travels or, through marriage, shifted their allegiance to another village, the result would be disastrous. Unless the simple and very logical rules of the game were followed, women would suffer and villages die. No good Minang would allow that to happen.

Agus spoke again. "The customs of the people here differ from our own, Anis. Think of the saying 'neither softened by the rain nor cracked by the sun.' We must take care that such a thing does not happen."

Anis said nothing. His thoughts were far away.

"Have you any idea what this would do to your mother?" Agus asked. "If you were to marry someone from here, your children, your grandchildren, would be *anak pisang*, sprouts growing outside the fence of your garden. They would be children without inheritance and, as the saying goes, 'neither adding to nor decreasing the family account.'"

Anis respected Agus and did not argue with him. He knew that what Agus said was true but in this case the right way was wrong. That had been proven to him in November of the previous year when he had returned home for what he now hoped was his last time.

Frustrated and upset but with a little money from Ujang, Anis had had no choice but to take the train home. He hadn't wanted to take Ujang's money but there had been no other option. He vowed that he would pay back the money on his return. He arrived at the train station in Bukittinggi very early in the morning but because of the declining condition of the railways under the Japanese the train for Padangpanjang didn't leave until eleven o'clock. There in Padangpanjang, he had to wait another few hours, until evening, for the train to Solok to arrive. It was past six o'clock when he arrived in Kacang and from there he had to walk two and a half hours to his village in the mountains to the east. He didn't arrive home until long after dark.

Anis' mother greeted him with shrieks and tears. The neighbors came and Anis was served an extra-special meal. He wasn't allowed to sleep at home, however. Under Minangkabau tradition, once a young man has come of age he may no longer sleep in his mother's home. Besides, his sister was married and her husband now lived at the house. Anis slept at the village's *surau*, the small religious training center. It was there he learned of Yulidar's marriage.

"Yulidar is married," Anis said to his mother accusingly when he returned home in the morning to eat. His sister's husband was gone. At home were his mother, his sister, and her two small children.

"Eat, then I will tell you what happened," his mother said to him.

"Tell me first," Anis answered shortly. His mother told him what had happened: "Everyone here thought you were dead, Anis. Last year, during the fasting month, Yulidar was asked for. Her uncle came to me and asked me for my permission. What could I say? She married shortly thereafter. I attended the wedding. But, Anis, how could anyone know you were still alive?"

Anis said nothing. There was nothing for him to say. His mother had behaved as tradition had demanded. His mother that morning was different from the mother who had welcomed him home the night before, her eyes brimming with tears of emotion and affection.

His uncle, his mother's younger brother and the man ultimately responsible for his care, came to cheer him up but Anis was far beyond the point of consolation.

"Sutan Sati came to my house this morning," his uncle informed him.

Anis said nothing.

"His niece Ros is older now and he said, if you agree, he would be willing to put in a good word for you. Think it over. It's not often around here that the woman's side takes the initiative in a marriage proposal. This is a great honor for our family."

Anis still said nothing.

"If you don't find Ros agreeable, then wait for a month or so. There are at least three girls here that I could help you get to take Yulidar's place. If you don't want to accept my help, you can stop calling me 'uncle.'"

Anis paid no attention whatsoever to his uncle's comments. The middle-aged man soon understood that his presence was not appreciated and left.

After his uncle left Anis spoke with his mother. "Ujang told me that he gave my money to you."

"It's gone; it was used to buy clothing and jewelry for your niece," his mother answered honestly.

According to tradition, that is what his money was for. His obligation as an uncle was to pay for the needs of his sister's children. In fact, if he were to die they would inherit his wealth and possessions. What could he say?

Now, in Pakanbaru, he couldn't be bothered with Agus' advice.

"There's another saying," Anis began carefully, hoping not to offend his friend: " 'The place that feeds you is the place you should call home.' You know, Agus, if I never go home again, that will be all right with me. God created the entire world. Why should one place be better than another?"

The two men said nothing for a time. Agus, who knew Anis' life history, addressed his friend cautiously.

"Our language is filled with proverbs and sayings. These are the guidelines of our *adat*, our tradition. According to the saying, heaven lies beneath your mother's feet. You've heard the story of Malin Kundang. Think of the moral of that story. Do nothing to cause one's mother distress."

"But, for me, the story of Malin Kundang has another meaning as well. Malin left his village with only rags on his back but returned wearing gold-embroidered robes and with a beautiful wife and a ship full of riches. Isn't that the aspiration of each and every *perantau?* That in the end Malin Kundang was cursed by his mother and changed into stone was the result of his own stupidity and misfortune. His mother didn't put a curse on him because he married a foreign woman, did she?"

❀

Sergeant Kiguchi had his own recipe for dealing with problems and there was no better time to try it than now, when Lieutenant Ose was in Pakanbaru and authority over the camp was in his hands. What he saw as a problem was in fact very simple. The detainees were not being treated in the way that prisoners of war should be treated. Maybe the war would end soon but the detainees were still prisoners and should be treated as such.

After roll call on that Wednesday evening the Dutch internees were kept standing in place. Freddie was ordered to give the men their bowls and to serve their food. He had no help because Kliwon still hadn't returned to camp after escorting Lieutenant Ose to the station. After eating their meal in standing position, the Dutch, including Freddie, were herded back to the rail embankment that was undergoing repair.

This kind of treatment was new to the men. Usually, in Lieutenant Ose's absence they were slapped and kicked. This new method caused their hair to stand on end. The Japanese soldiers accompanied them to the embankment, carrying with them cots and cooking utensils. The first order the men were given was to gather firewood. Immediately the Dutch set off into the rubber estate where, since it was the middle of the dry season, there was an abundance of firewood. The Dutch were then allowed to watch the Japanese light a fire, open their tins of food, and devour the food ravenously.

The seven-day moon hung high and clear in the cloudless sky. A soft wind carried with it the cool night air. Some of the Dutch were ordered to set up torches around the site where they gathered earth for landfill. The Dutch were able to guess what it was they were to do that night. Soon after a bell began to ring, signaling that it was ten o'clock Tokyo time. The Japanese hadn't forgotten to bring along their clock, which was placed on the ground near the fire, and a piece of rail, which was hung from the branch of a rubber tree near the embankment.

Kiguchi shouted for the men to line up. The well-muscled sergeant stood in front of the row. He put his hands out before him and divided the row in two. He swung his left arm to the side, a signal for the men on his left. "Sleep!" he cried out. He then swung his right arm to the side. "Work!" he ordered.

The Dutch seemed confused at first but soon understood what they were to do. The Japanese soldiers moved in and began to herd the two groups toward their respective places: those who were to work, down to the bottom of the embankment, and those who were to sleep, over to the base of the bridge.

The night was beautiful and calm. The sky was clear. The moon, so bright that the other stars brave enough to appear that night paled in comparison, began to move slowly toward the west. The gentle night wind rustled the tops of the rubber trees. The dried reeds on the banks of the river became a chain of gold. Beneath the silver moonlight the wooden trestle looked old but strong. The river below, narrowed by the heat of the dry season, moved slowly along, catching and reflecting like a gold-scaled fish the light of the moon that hung in the sky. The sound of night animals mixed with the rustling of the reeds and was occasionally heightened by the cry of birds flying abreast through the night sky. Then the sound of shovels, the footsteps of the detainees, and another load of earth put into place.

Across the river and slightly upstream was the flickering light of lamps and torches in the mosque and village homes. A few of the villagers were walking away from the mosque, their *tarawih* prayers finished.

Wimpie was in the group that was to sleep first but he sat taking in the situation around him. All the Dutch were present, half of them working, half of them asleep, but no one was attempting to disturb the night's silence with his voice. The Japanese were there too, sleeping, roasting something to eat on the open fire, or standing guard. No one spoke. Everyone to a man was lost in his own concerns.

The men on the first work shift were exhausted but tried to appear as if they were working hard. They had already spent three and a half years in detention under the Japanese and their survival alone was proof that they had learned how to exercise strict control over their bodies and how to work efficiently yet expend a minimal amount of energy. In regular fashion, one man following another, they went up the eastern side of the embankment with baskets of earth on their shoulders to empty them on the western side.

Wimpie thought that the rest of the men in his group, the second shift, were asleep. He was wrong. One other man was awake. That was Pastor who lay uneasily on the hard earth and railroad ties. Wimpie stared at him. Their eyes met.

"I feel sorry for them," Pastor said.

"Feel sorry for yourself," Wimpie advised. "It's going to be your turn to work next."

"But at least we've had a chance to sleep, to rest up, haven't we?"

"Who's slept? You haven't slept. I haven't slept either."

"Is something bothering you, Wimpie?" Pastor asked him after being silent for a time.

"No. Go to sleep."

"Are you upset because your plan's ruined?"

"My plan is not ruined. We can escape tomorrow for sure."

"But this delay is not a good sign."

Wimpie watched Pastor closely. One blow would be sufficient to put him to sleep for the rest of the night. The Japanese wouldn't know. He put the thought out of his head.

"Quite a number of the men have said they want to go along, but in time I think they'll back out. Believe me. There's not a man among us with the guts to do it. That we're all internees is proof of that."

"It was my impression that our discussion on this matter was closed last night," Wimpie told Pastor. Now he really did feel like slugging the man.

"You'll never make it through the jungle alone," Pastor added.

"If you and the rest want to stay here and serve the Japanese, that is up to you. But I'm going to escape, even if I have to do it alone."

"You'll be trapped in the jungle for the rest of your very short life. The war will end and we will leave this camp as victors."

"Victors? And just what is it that you have done to help win this war, Pastor? Follow the orders of the Japanese and help them build their railroad?" Wimpie made no attempt to check his sarcasm.

The two men were silent. Wimpie stretched out and tried to sleep. He was tired and the night, cool and quiet with its light wind, lent an air of security. Every now and then a night bird passed, its flight marked by the soft whoosh of its wings. Afterward, silence once more. Every once in a while a fish would jump from the water to catch an insect. A splash and then silence once more. It was still too early to sleep.

Pastor van Roscott couldn't sleep either. He felt nervous

and afraid, especially now when thinking about sleeping alone in the barracks the following night. It was so strange. He felt sure that the war would be over soon. In a different situation and with a more respected position he might be able to say that he had received an inspiration and people would not only believe him, they would praise his insight and wisdom.

When the bell sounded again, signaling that it was twelve o'clock Tokyo time, the two men were still awake. The Dutch who had been working were quickly gathered together and counted. One of the soldiers approached the men who were sleeping, woke them, and ordered them to begin work. Well trained, the detainees awoke and immediately went to work, except for Pastor van Roscott who continued to lie on the ground pretending to be asleep.

The soldier went up to him and kicked him awake and into sitting position.

"Work!" the soldier screamed.

The soldier's cry caught everyone's attention, including that of Sergeant Kiguchi. Everyone stood at a distance but continued to watch.

Now is the time, Pastor thought. In educated Malay and a clear and practiced speaking voice he shouted: "You Japanese are acting inhumanly and disobeying the rules of the Geneva Convention. These men have been working all day; now they need to sleep."

From where he stood Wimpie shouted in Dutch: "Van Roscott! What are you doing? Do you want to get yourself killed?" He began to run toward van Roscott but halfway there was blocked by Kiguchi who was standing beside his cot. Kiguchi struck at Wimpie with his arm but Wimpie was fast. Avoiding the blow, he ran to pick up his basket for carrying earth and grabbing it, went scurrying down the embankment.

Kiguchi made no attempt to chase Wimpie. He stood in place, continuing to stare at Pastor. The incident had come as a surprise to the soldier assigned to wake the internees and now he stood in complete confusion looking back and forth at Kiguchi and Pastor.

Pastor began once more: "These Dutch internees are people, not animals . . ." He stopped, remembering that none of the Japanese could understand. At best they might know twenty words in Bahasa Indonesia among them, most of which were vulgar, having been learned and used during leave time in Pakanbaru.

The other Dutch internees in the second shift began to work. Pastor grew nervous; all the Japanese were watching him. Meanwhile, the detainees who had just completed the first shift of work were coming back and lying down to sleep. Not one of them addressed him.

The soldier standing near Pastor was also nervous. He went to the man and pulled him up into standing position. "Work!" he screamed.

Pastor sat back down. Kiguchi did not react at all. The soldier became more sure of himself. He pulled Pastor into standing position. "Work!" he screamed again as he landed a hefty blow on the Dutchman's cheek. Pastor went flying backward. Kiguchi still showed no reaction. "You are animals," Pastor cried out before sitting down once more.

Although surprised and sympathetic, the other detainees said nothing as they watched the incident unfold before them.

The Japanese soldier became even more self-assured. He pulled Pastor back into standing position, kicked him in the groin, and with the back of his right hand struck him across the left side of his face as he doubled over in pain. Pastor stumbled toward the edge of the embankment, then fell, tumbling about three meters to the hard earth below.

Two of the Japanese soldiers went after Pastor and putting his arms over their shoulders, began to carry him back to the top. Wimpie came up to help them.

"What are you doing, Pastor?" he whispered in Dutch.

Pastor said nothing. He wasn't unconscious but he groaned in pain. Every bone in his body felt broken. He was surprised that none were. More surprising, none of his bones were even out of joint.

Kiguchi met the men at the embankment's edge. He lifted Pastor and alone carried him to the place where the detainees were to sleep. There, he laid him gently on the ground.

"Sleep!" he ordered the man.

The situation calmed down once more. Half the Dutch were at work, the other half asleep. The Japanese soldiers went back to what they had been doing earlier. Pastor lay alone in his thoughts, unable to sleep. His whole body ached but what hurt most was his pride. His plans had ended in total failure. He had not become a hero; in fact, none of the other detainees had even shown him any sympathy. Worse yet, they thought him crazy! And now because he was permitted to sleep, they could accuse him of thinking only about himself. He felt the distance that separated him from the other detainees grow wider.

When the bell rang twice the shift changed again but Pastor was allowed to sleep undisturbed. He couldn't sleep, however, and lay awake full of unease, regret, and disappointment.

When the bell rang four times, the shift was changed again, this time for the last time. At six o'clock Tokyo time the men were herded back to the barracks.

There the Pastor lay awake.

❧

After the completion of *asar* prayers Haji Zen remained at the mosque for further prayers. While praying he thought he saw out of the corner of his eye a familiar shape walking beside the mosque in the direction of the market. It wasn't even seven o'clock so it would be normal for people to be out and about, especially today, a market day, but most people would be walking away from the market, not toward it. Haji Zen paused in his prayers for a second; the person walking toward the market must have been Hasan. But no, it couldn't have been. Hasan was waiting at the crossing place for Kliwon and the Dutch detainees, wasn't he? Haji

Zen finished his closing prayer in haste, wiped his face with his palms, and then left the mosque through the back portico. His eyes scanned the footpath that led to the market. He hoped to see someone other than Hasan on the path but not a single person was visible.

No, it couldn't have been Hasan, he thought again.

Haji Zen stood for some time inside the back portico of the mosque, completely lost in thought. He had just given Kliwon his blessing to go, probably for the last time. Inside he began to feel that he had made a mistake. What if Kliwon were killed in the jungle? He felt shame as well. Indirectly or not, hadn't he supported Kliwon's decision to leave? And hadn't he done so because he thought—although he wasn't sure—that Anis intended to propose to Lena? Even if Anis did propose who was to know whether Lena would accept?

He had heard a great deal about the customs of the Minangkabau, not much of it very good. Most significant, Minangkabau men often took more than one wife. In addition, they always sent their earnings home to the village they came from. If this were true of Anis then he was certainly not a good match for Lena. There would never be peace in their house and even his own wealth would be threatened. At the same time, the Minangkabau were good traders and Anis himself seemed to be sympathetic and honest.

Haji Zen heard the shrill cry of a locomotive whistle. Not much later, the cargo train from Sijunjung to Pakanbaru began to make its way over the bridge. Haji Zen walked slowly home.

Kliwon didn't go back to camp after the train left. He knew that without Lieutenant Ose around, Sergeant Kiguchi would find an outlet for his pent-up anger. It would be best for him to avoid the place altogether. Trying to escape that night was now out of the question. Kiguchi was strict about security. The Dutch were well aware of this as well. The look in their eyes as they watched him carry Lieutenant Ose's knapsack convinced him of that.

Kliwon went directly from the station to Haji Zen's house where he found him standing out front.

"We're not leaving tonight," Kliwon informed Haji Zen after greeting him.

"What?" Haji Zen asked, his face showing surprise and a trace of happiness and disappointment as well. How was he to react to this? he wondered.

"Lieutenant Ose has gone to Pakanbaru," Kliwon added.

"Oh," Haji Zen said nonplussed, not understanding the connection between the delay in escape plans and the departure of the lieutenant.

"Sergeant Kiguchi, who takes over for him when he goes, is vicious. We couldn't make a peep without his knowing."

Haji Zen now began to understand and saw a chance to regain his composure.

"Yes, you must be careful and not do anything that could jeopardize your well-being."

"If Lieutenant Ose comes back we'll probably leave tomorrow."

"Come on in the house," Haji Zen said.

"I'd like to say my *asar* prayers first; there's not much time left," Kliwon said as he went down to the raft to wash himself in preparation for prayers.

A prayer rug was always to be found in the middle room of Haji Zen's house, the floor of which was covered by rattan mats. That is where Kliwon said his prayers. After finishing, Kliwon looked up to see that Haji Zen's family had gathered in the room and were waiting for him in silence.

"So, your escape has been postponed?" Haji Deramah asked.

"Yes," Kliwon answered simply.

"Maybe it's a sign. Maybe you shouldn't try to run away at all," she added.

"Yes, Kliwon. Why do you have to run away?" Lena asked.

Now Kliwon was sure. He was convinced that with Lena as his wife, a bright and promising future awaited him. Only Wimpie stood in the way. Were he to hide, Wimpie would somehow, someday find him. Freddie knew about

Haji Zen's house. Staying there was out of the question. And if the Dutch decided against trying to escape? Work on the embankment was almost finished and they would soon return to Pakanbaru. There, Wimpie would find Siti's husband who would then come looking for him. Or if Siti's husband had divorced her, she herself might come after him.

Kliwon stayed at the house until it was time for breaking fast, all the while parrying the women's pleas that he not try to escape. Haji Zen said little to him during this time, neither urging him to stay nor pressuring him to run.

After breaking fast, they left the house together. Haji Zen and his family were off to the mosque for *tarawih* prayers; Kliwon was going back to the camp. Outside the door to the house they stopped. Across the river the Dutch were working beneath the light of rubber torches.

"Are you sure you want to go back?" Haji Zen inquired.

"Come along with us," Lena urged.

For a moment Kliwon didn't know what to do.

"I think I'll wait here until it looks like things are back to normal. Then I'll go back to camp."

After Haji Zen and his family left, Kliwon walked to the top of the trestle so he could see what was happening. He decided not to return to his barracks and stretched out on the embankment where he fell directly asleep.

Kliwon was awaked by the commotion across the river. He watched Pastor being beaten by one of the Japanese soldiers and saw Kiguchi carry the unfortunate man back to the place where the other men were sleeping.

The village side of the Kampar Kanan River was silent. The older people were sure to be asleep. Haji Zen and Haji Deramah would have returned from the mosque some time ago. They would be asleep by now. A light still glowed in the mosque. The young men had stayed behind for *tadarusan*. He doubted whether the young women had gone home either.

It was still. The sky was clear and the seven-day moon hung high in the western sky. Something inside drove him back toward the mosque to wait for Lena.

Long after hearing the bell ring once he saw Lena leaving

the field that doubled as a market and head toward home. Kliwon went to greet her.

Even from a distance Lena could tell that the man coming toward her was Kliwon. The Dutch were still working. Kliwon had not returned. By the light of the moon she could see that Kliwon still had the parcel she had given him in his hands. By village standards Lena was a bit too free and easygoing and she stopped beside her house to wait for Kliwon.

"So, you didn't go back to camp after all," she said to him.

"I wasn't about to go back after the Japanese beat up one of the Dutchmen."

"They beat a man up?" Lena asked while looking at the activity across the river. The Dutch appeared to be working calmly and without interruption. She couldn't detect any unrest.

"It happened about an hour ago," Kliwon informed her. "They pushed him off the embankment."

"Did he die?"

"I don't know."

"Hold this for me, Kliwon," Lena said as she handed him her torch. "I have to make a stop down there before going in. Don't you follow me now."

Kliwon immediately doused the torch and followed Lena to the raft. Lena said nothing. Kliwon sat down on the deck to wait. From where he sat the Dutch detainees were not visible. Attached to the raft at a slant, the thatch wall he had his back to prevented people across the river from seeing in but did not obstruct people who were using the raft from taking water from the river.

Lena returned to Kliwon and sat down beside him on the raft.

"Why do you insist on going, Kliwon?" she asked him.

Kliwon seemed confused. "For my own safety, Lena. Do you want to see me tortured by the Japanese?"

"But you'll come back here, won't you?" the young woman said after a moment.

"As soon as possible," Kliwon assured her. "The next

time Pak Hasan makes a trip to that village I'll come back with him."

"You'll come to see us, won't you?"

"If your mother and father have no objections, I will stay here forever," he told her. "I love you, Lena," he added almost inaudibly.

That was it. That was the sentence he had read in so many stories and heard in so many tales. That was the sentence the young man was supposed to say and the sentence the young woman was supposed to want to hear when the proper moment arrived. Oddly enough, when the moment did arrive it was not an easy thing to say. As a weapon though, the sentence was a most effective one, capable of breaking down whatever barriers existed between the speaker and the person spoken to.

"Oh, Kliwon," Lena sighed while pressing her body against his. Kliwon embraced her tightly and kissed her face, then her lips. Lena felt embarrassed and surprised but allowed him to continue.

When Kliwon's hand continued its search of her body she said only, "Don't, Kliwon," but with little real protest. What defenses she had were now destroyed.

At the sound of the drum, the signal for *sahur*, Lena freed herself from Kliwon. Hurriedly, she put on her clothes that were scattered around the raft and without a word ran up the bank and to her house. She stole around the house and entered through the unlocked back door. She felt confused and uncertain. Her body ached with a mixture of pain and pleasure. Alone now, Kliwon felt his entire body shivering with happiness and fear. He dressed slowly and then walked back to the railway trestle. Across the river, the Dutch were still working. He lay down but it was quite some time before he finally fell asleep.

❧

It wasn't until after eight thirty that Wednesday evening that the train carrying Lieutenant Ose and the other Japanese commanders rolled into Rintis Station in Pakanbaru.

By that time, the announcement from *Tennō Heika* that the Dai Nippon Army was to cease all forms of aggression against the Allied forces was more than eight hours old and had begun to make its impact felt in all corners of the world. Ose and the other officers on the train knew nothing about this but they were not impervious to the strangeness in the air that afternoon. Not a word was spoken throughout the trip. No one, it seemed, dared to comment on the strange thing that each and every one observed: there were no Dutch prisoners of war at work. As the journey continued a terrible weight slowly but surely began to grow inside each man on the train. The weight threatened to pull them down, to drown them in deep and dark uncertainty. In an instant they would be gone. Without a word spoken, without a word among them, they became sure of the outcome of the Greater East Asian War. Slowly, this awareness began to kill them.

No one was at the station to meet them.

On foot, the distance between the Pakanbaru station and the military headquarters could be covered in a half hour but the road passed through the center of the town and the trip seemed to drag on forever. Although it was dark, no one spoke. The men walked in a daze, their open eyes taking in the view of the quiet city. Although together, they walked alone, each of the men keeping pace with his own thoughts. The feeling of aloneness, of utter silence, overcame them.

The soldier in the guardhouse that stood in front of military headquarters saluted as they passed but no one was in the security post at the side. A twenty-five-watt bulb attempted to illuminate the room's interior but succeeded only in heightening the appearance of complete emptiness. In the yard, a number of soldiers were sitting on the ground beneath the hazy light that emanated from the security post. A few stared at the officers as they passed with their knapsacks in hand; the others didn't even look at them.

What everyone feared had taken place. This was their common thought. But reality, Ose mused, was not as frightening as he had imagined.

The security post commander came running out to greet them and, after saluting, directed them to their accommodations, two rooms in the former primary school.

"Did we lose?" one of the officers asked.

"I have not been informed, Major," the security commander, a sergeant, answered respectfully.

The other officers stared at the man who had asked the question. While that same question had occupied almost their every thought since afternoon or, in fact since the night before, it should not have been asked. Asking it, verbalizing it, was a stupid and disrespectful thing to do. The question was sacred. They had awaited and, at the same time, feared its answer for so long but knew that if they were patient and showed the proper respect they would soon receive the answer from the person with the authority to give it to them. Not a mere sergeant!

The officer who had asked the question did not have to look at the faces of his colleagues to know what they were thinking. He sensed their disapproval and immediately felt ashamed.

"I'm sorry," he said nervously and to no one in particular. No one regarded his apology.

The wall that once separated the two six-by-eight-meter classrooms had been taken down and now there were eighteen beds arranged neatly in the expanded space. Twelve of the small beds were positioned, one next to another, along the sixteen-meter wall opposite the entrance to the room. Each bed was made up with a set of white sheets and had a pillow atop it and a small chest at its foot. Closer to the door, toward the center of the room, was a long dining table with benches and on the wall beside the entranceway was another row of six beds. Apparent from the bags atop them and items on the bureaus, some of the beds had already been claimed by the officers who had arrived earlier. Dishes of food lay on the dining table.

"You have approximately one-half hour to prepare and eat before being called," announced the sergeant who had met them. He then saluted and left.

Each of the officers took a bed. Except for Ose, few of the men had slept in this dormitory. When they were in Pakanbaru most of the men stayed at the homes of staff officers or spent their nights at the bordello that had been established for their use. The men said nothing about having to stay in the dormitory and took their beds without complaint. Every man had a bed but three of the beds were empty.

While waiting to be met, Lieutenant Ose went to the communications room and asked to be put through to Taratakbuluh. No answer. Ose asked the two soldiers who manned the room to try to reach Taratakbuluh again and, if the call were answered, to have it transferred to the auditorium of the residency.

Some of the officers were crying—that was their first impression upon entering the auditorium. It was over for sure, they thought sadly, but with a bit of relief as well. As unobtrusively as possible, the late arrivals took their places among the other officers already present. In all, forty men were there. Camp commanders sat at three of the four tables that had been positioned in a rectangular shape in the middle of the room while on the fourth side of the rectangle sat the commander in chief for the Riau Regional Command and his staff members.

The auditorium was large and well illuminated by electric lights. The paintings and other decorative objects that had once filled the walls had long ago been taken down. Now on the wall behind the commander in chief was the *Hinomaru*, the Japanese flag. Ose's eyes searched the room. He wasn't there; Major Shinji was not present.

They waited for a long time. But for the suppressed sobbing of some officers, the room was silent. The telephone rang and was answered by the adjutant who put his ear to the receiver to listen. Ose waited anxiously.

"*Asso-ka!* Is that so?" the adjutant spoke into the receiver. That was all he said before putting the receiver back in place.

It was 2100 Tokyo time.

The commander in chief finally awoke from his thoughts,

whereupon he turned to the adjutant and asked: "Is everyone present?"

"Except for the two men who committed *seppuku,*" the adjutant answered. All eyes were on him.

"Who?"

"Major Shinji and Captain Matsuda."

Ose's mouth dropped open.

The commander in chief appeared to attach no great significance to the information. He looked at each of the men present, one after another.

"Gentlemen," he said slowly and authoritatively. The silence in the room grew deeper. The men who had been crying did their best to stifle their sobs. Completely out of custom, the commander in chief remained seated as he opened the meeting.

"At twelve o'clock today *Tennō Heika* himself announced the unconditional surrender of Japan and ordered the Dai Nippon Army to cease all forms of aggression against the Allied forces and further, until the arrival of the proper representative of the Allied forces, to maintain control over local security and administration of the government."

All of the men present knew what the commander in chief would say even before he said it but the way in which he spoke, the simple and straightforward nature of his announcement, raised in them a sense of emotion they had not felt before. They were in a dream. This wasn't happening. The incident the commander spoke of was far away in another world, another period of time, and had nothing to do with themselves. Only gradually did the reality of the situation begin to sink into their consciousness.

A major rose from his seat and made a half bow in the direction of the commander in chief or possibly *Hinoramu* on the wall behind him. He then made another half bow toward the other men in the room and took a few steps backward. Calmly, he withdrew his sword from its scabbard at his waist and turned it so that it was pointed toward his heart. He pulled the sword toward him forcefully but not forcefully enough. He threw his body forward. He did not cry out. Only a small moan escaped from his throat. Then his body began to convulse, like a chicken with its head cut off.

No one attempted to stop the man's struggling as he fell and twisted and squirmed like a fish thrown from the water onto land. Very few paid attention.

The adjutant stood and weakly shouted an order for attention. All present obeyed.

"We will sing the *Kimigayo*," the man said and then sounded the proper pitch.

The men sang the national anthem, a hymn-like song, twice. Tears dripped down most of the men's cheeks. But not the commander in chief's; not Ose's either.

Ose's thoughts flew far away to his home village and back to a different incident in another time that now seemed only a dream. It was all so blurred. The strains of the *Kimigayo* vanished and were replaced by those of another song from another time: Osaka, one evening in mid summer, 2600 *Showa*. The music accompanying the troop ship as it left the dock was parade music, military songs that promised victory, heroism and glory for all.

A aa, ano kao de, ano ko-e-de,
Tegara tanomu to tsuma ya koga

A wistful face and trembling voice
Await your return and medals on your chest.

Michiko stood on the dock, one among the thousands of others who had come to say good-bye. She was dressed in white, the color of fidelity, and carrying their new baby, born only a few months before. Standing stiffly at her side was the family of the poor postman. His father hadn't changed his postal uniform. His mother held Ose's first son in her arms. Beside her were his two older sisters whose husbands were already on the battlefield.

Exactly one year later, at the end of Ose's home leave, the incident was repeated. This time, however, his mother held the youngest. The older boy stood hand in hand with his grandfather, the old postman in his uniform.

106

When the ship left that first time in the summer of 2600 Ose felt that the beautiful song he heard that day had been written especially for him. Neither he nor Michiko however had proved capable of fulfilling the hopes it expressed. Michiko didn't wait and he came back with no medals.

Kimigayo ended and was punctuated by the sound of a gunshot. As the song ended another major placed the barrel of his gun to his temple and pulled the trigger. The officer beside him was splattered by blood and pieces of bone and brain but he remained, not moving, in place. A few heads turned for a moment. That was the only reaction.

The commander in chief began to speak: "Remember. . . ." He stopped, unable to continue. Remember what? "A moment of silence," he said simply.

The moment ended.

The commander in chief opened the folio that was lying on the table in front of him and read the orders of *Tennō Heika*, then those of the commander of the Far East Forces in Singapore and those of his own office, the Riau Regional Command. The orders were short and clear.

The adjutant led the men in the singing of *Kimigayo* once more, then ordered the men at ease. The officers sat down. The officer who had been hit by the spray of flesh and blood took a handkerchief from his pocket and quickly wiped off his face and clothing. The other men sat in silence, showing no reaction, appearing to be absent of all thought. Ose looked around him.

Shinji. How had he done it? With his pistol or his sword? More than likely with his pistol. Shinji was more rash than brave but comparing himself with Shinji, Ose was clearly a coward. The starting point of Shinji's life had been tradition. He himself had been forced to search for tradition.

Ever since they had met and become classmates and friends at the technical school, Ose had seen Shinji as the ideal Japanese man. Shinji was bigger, stronger, more carefree, and much better versed in Japan's cultural history. Shinji seemed to have the answer to every problem. They had become friends and when Shinji decided to take *sumo* lessons he invited Ose to join.

"But I am studying *judo*," Ose told him.

"*Judo?*" Shinji asked, somewhat surprised. "Why *judo?*"

"Practice is near home," Ose answered. Actually, he was only taking lessons because his father had ordered him to. According to his father, *judo* would give him courage.

"Well, I know that *judo* is good for you," Shinji, a master of argument, began. "But *judo* is for this world. *Sumo* is the game of the gods and represents the teachings of *Kami*. That's why *sumo* is taught in temples."

"Oh, I think they're all pretty much the same."

"On the contrary. But if you can master both *judo* and *sumo* you'll be a man not easily dismissed by anyone."

Shinji's reasons for studying *sumo* sounded convincing enough and Ose began to practice regularly. It was Shinji who didn't.

Yes, he had probably killed himself with a pistol.

The adjutant approached the soldier standing guard at the door and whispered something to him. The guard left and then a short while later came back with other soldiers who proceeded to carry away the bodies of the two men. No one seemed to take notice. More soldiers came in carrying trays of beer, saké, and cakes.

The men drank in robot-like fashion, not saying a word. Their faces showed no emotion whatsoever. One drink followed another.

One of the men began to sing. An army marching song. The others joined in. Then a navy song. Everyone sang but with no spirit. They seemed to be trying to remember whether these songs, which they had once sung with such zest, had any relevance to reality at all. One song followed another. Another drink. Nothing was spoken. Another song, another drink.

Some of the men placed their heads on the table. They continued to sing but with little tone or rhythm. A pause, another drink, another song.

The process continued through the night. No other men committed *hara-kiri*. No others tried.

At five o'clock in the morning Tokyo time the soldiers

came back into the room again, this time to carry the officers one by one out of the auditorium. The officers were placed in their automobiles or in buses. The vehicles then pulled out of the residency yard.

Aruke, aruke, aruke,
Minami o kita e.

One two, one two, one two,
We march to the north and to the south.

THREE

Tam, tam buku
Berleret anak lima,
Patah ranting, patah paku,
Anak b'lakang tangkap satu.

A tisket, a tasket
A green and yellow basket
Sent a letter to my love,
But on the way I lost it.

At the time Satiyah was born, Mersi was just a rural area
on the edge of the city of Purwokerto in the regency of
Banyumas, central Java. Of course, when Satiyah was born,
Purwokerto was not yet the regency's seat. Up until the
time she had been forced to leave, Mersi was a calm, peaceful, and orderly village. The only thing out of the ordinary
to have happened in Mersi and about which people still
talked was that Surti, a girl from the village, had been made
the mistress of a white man from Purwokerto.

Beautiful images from the past often crept into Satiyah's
consciousness when she wasn't working, just as they did
that Thursday morning, August 16, 2605, after she had
finished eating her early morning meal.

Satiyah awoke with the distant sound of four bells. It was
time for *sahur*. The camp was exceptionally quiet but she
could hear a commotion in the distance. She peeked out
through a crack in the thatch wall. Darkness. She couldn't
see anything. The moon had set and the torches were not in

their customary places. She felt as if she were in another world.

Peering harder she made out the light of torches on the railway embankment. The Dutch detainees who had earlier in the evening been herded back to the embankment by Sergeant Kiguchi were still hard at work.

Satiyah moved about carefully, anxious not to disturb the purity of the room's silence. After finishing her early morning meal she found herself unable to fall back to sleep because of recurring images of Mersi. She allowed the images to come back even though she knew they would end with a picture of shame, the reason she had been forced to leave the village and why she might never return again.

The climax of Satiyah's life in Mersi was her marriage with Ndoro Alimin. Her life with him was a good one, especially if measured by the standards of the lower class of Mersi into which she had been born. As a teacher, Alimin's salary was far larger than that of a level-three machinist at the Seraju Dal Spoorweg Maatschapij. Satiyah's household income was far greater than most other girls her age could even imagine.

After the coming of the Japanese, the situation changed and Alimin's real wage shrank to a size not even sufficient to live on for a week. Nonetheless, Satiyah's life remained a somewhat favored one because, quite unimaginably, her father was able to supplement his income through profits from small trade carried out on the train. Under the Japanese, railroad engineers suddenly became people of account. They were able to reap relatively large profits from trade in hard-to-get goods, including rice. There was always a corner somewhere on the train in which to secrete goods that would escape the notice of the inspector. A steam locomotive is such a complex piece of equipment that the machinists were able to ensure that hidden cargo would not be detected.

With monetary assistance from her mother, Satiyah had few complaints. Although Ndoro Alimin was still unable to fulfill his physical duties as a husband, Satiyah didn't let herself dwell on such matters. Their two children took up most of her time and attention. For Alimin, however, living off contributions from Satiyah's family was not acceptable so Satiyah began to engage in small trade. The difficult conditions of the Japanese occupation forced almost everyone to seek extra sources of income. There was always one item or another that people were unable to obtain and anyone with the right connections or with access to hard-to-come-by goods immediately went into trade. At that time there was need for a large range of goods: new and used clothing, quinine pills, arsphenamine, nutmeg, sugar, coffee, kerosene, cooking oil, virtually anything, but the trade commodity of greatest value was rice.

Under the Japanese, rice was taken directly from the farmers by Japanese soldiers or their helpers. Farmers were forced to devise increasingly clever means of hiding their rice for later sale to black market traders. As for the traders, they were no less clever and soon established mutually satisfactory ties with drivers, train engineers, and other such people who because of the trade were able to supplement their often meager wages.

The cooperative ties that were established for the sale of black market goods proved to be extremely efficient. The Japanese set up numerous inspection posts but the bulk of contraband goods slipped by their watchful eyes. The black market expanded rapidly and soon Satiyah made the plunge too. She enjoyed an advantage not available to many others: she rarely had to pay to ride the train. Because she was known by almost all the train workers as the daughter of a machinist she was able to gain their trust and assistance much more easily than other traders could.

Almost every day Satiyah left her house to take the train to villages along the railroad line. She took with her goods that farmers and villagers needed and traded them for goods that were hard to find in Purwokerto. In the evening she would arrive home, always tired but also satisfied from knowing that she was able to supply her family with needed provisions. Unlike the vast majority of people who were forced to fill their stomachs with corn, cassava, soybeans, and other inexpensive kinds of food, her family always had rice. Her family's life was fairly tranquil. Although Ndoro Alimin still found the situation less than ideal, at the very least his family was no longer dependent on handouts.

A common expression is that a deer will sometimes forget a trap but a trap will never forget the deer. Misran was a name that Satiyah had erased from her memory. After her marriage to Alimin, Satiyah had put Misran out of existence. Misran was a man who had once almost ruined her life and her escape from that fate was something she never ceased to be thankful for. It was odd then that she allowed herself to forget about Misran.

Misran was the boil on the face of Mersi. He had no education to speak of and spent most of his time engaged in petty crime in the city, from which he obtained the money that he spent in the village. Most of the people of Mersi looked with scorn on Misran's parents. Some ridiculed them; others pitied them. But whatever they felt about his parents, it was Misran they avoided.

The Japanese era began and the world turned upside down. Good, upstanding people like Ndoro Alimin and Ndoro Siman, the principal of Angka Loro School, faced destitution while people of little account prior to the coming of the Japanese saw their stars rise. Satiyah's father was one example. Misran was another. Misran, now a husband and a father, worked as an informant for the *Kenpeitai*, the Japanese secret police, in Purwokerto. During the Japanese period, the work of an informant was not something carried out in stealth, and because everyone knew who the informants were, the latter were able to do pretty much as they pleased. Informants learned to exploit the people's fear of the *Kenpeitai* to the maximum advantage.

"You are smuggling rice," Misran said to Satiyah, scaring her almost half out of her wits.

Satiyah had been waiting on the Mersi train platform that morning and Misran's presence had come as a complete surprise. She immediately remembered every detail of

113

the incident she had tried to forget. One evening, not too far from her home, Misran stopped her on the way back from the *warung*. Without even a word of greeting Misran embraced her and began to fondle her. Satiyah screamed as loud as she could and her cries brought people running from their homes. Misran was forced to flee.

Now who didn't know of and fear this man?

"How can you say that? I'm just selling odds and ends," Satiyah said in answer to his accusation.

"You're a liar and if you don't confess I'm going to have your husband dragged into the *Kenpeitai* office. You wouldn't want that to happen, would you?"

Satiyah's fear was written on her face and Misran knew that he had touched her most sensitive nerve.

"Get off the train in Sukorojo," Misran told her.

"But I'm not going to Sukorojo," Satiyah protested.

"Get off anyway and we'll discuss the matter there. I might be able to arrange some profitable trade for you."

"I'm doing fine on my own, Misran," Satiyah answered, trying to find a way out of the situation.

"I told you to get off in Sukorojo and that is where you are going to get off. If you don't, your husband is going to make a visit to the office."

Satiyah got off the train in Sukorojo. There was a sugar factory in Sukorojo but the route that Misran ordered her to follow was in the opposite direction. They walked for half an hour until finally arriving at a field. A small hut came into view and its sight alone was enough for Satiyah to know why Misran had brought her there. She was too afraid to refuse him but thought she might be able to arouse his sympathy through pleading and tears.

"Please, I have a husband and children," Satiyah told him as she stood outside the door.

"Come on in," Misran beckoned from inside. "We have things to talk about."

Satiyah's feet carried her through the door but once inside, she stopped.

"I don't want to force you," Misran told her. "I want you

114

to make the decision. You do what I want to do or I'll drag your husband in."

Misran was more despicable than she had imagined. He dressed just like a Japanese soldier and with one of his hands kept stroking the ends of his handlebar mustache.

Satiyah began to cry. Misran approached her and clutched her hand.

"Once, when I tried to do this, you screamed and set people running after me. Now think about my proposal . . ."

Misran began to stroke her breasts. Satiyah said nothing.

Satiyah felt disgusted with herself when she returned home that evening. She cried for so long that Alimin was forced to ask what was troubling her.

"My head hurts," she answered in reply to his questions.

"You must be tired. Stop working for a few days," he advised.

Alimin had paid little attention to Satiyah since his impotence and this helped her keep the incident with Misran a secret. She stayed home for a number of days but then, one day, Misran came to the door.

"I'll be waiting for you tomorrow," he told her and left without even a good-bye.

Unsure of what to do, Satiyah kept the appointment. She knew that what she was doing was wrong but also knew that if she didn't do it her husband would have to face a new round of torture. Misran was not a person to take lightly.

As time went by Satiyah began to enjoy her secret life. She continued, at regular intervals, to meet Misran until one day while she was waiting for the train a woman came running up to her shouting and screaming.

"Whore! You husband-stealing whore!"

It was that phrase she most remembered. The woman, Misran's wife, spat numerous other accusations at her as well. The whole platform was put in an uproar and Satiyah was forced to flee, leaving her goods behind.

About two hours later Ndoro Alimin came home accompanied by a crowd of people led by Misran's wife. He came into the house and went directly into the dining room where he sat down and stared into Satiyah's eyes. Outside, the people who had followed him home were making a horrible commotion. Everyone wanted to know what had happened.

"Is it true?" Alimin asked her.

Satiyah couldn't even reply. Tears were her only answer. Her husband remained where he was, continuing to stare. Even when she finally moved he remained where he was, his gaze fixed on the spot where she had been sitting.

Alimin did not move from his place that night, the next day, or the three days that followed. All talk in the village of Mersi centered on Satiyah's family. That was the only subject of conversation. Various means were tried in an attempt to bring Alimin back to consciousness. Numerous people were called in to help but to no avail. Alimin continued to sit in his chair, not eating, not drinking, not tending to his bodily needs, his eyes fixed on the spot where Satiyah had been when he came home. Satiyah's mother and father helped out by taking care of Satiyah's children. Ndoro Siman, the principal of Angka Loro School, also lent a hand. He came to the house every day to sit with Alimin and try to cheer him and rouse him back to consciousness. Nothing helped.

Around midday on the fourth day Alimin collapsed. Like a lamp without oil the light in his eyes faded. Those present carried him quickly into the bedroom and put him in his bed where he lay until early the next morning when he finally took his last breath.

A few days later Satiyah fled.

From the direction of the embankment came the sound of the bell ringing six times followed not long afterward by the tramping of the detainees being marched back to their barracks.

❧

A small watch post was located every five to ten kilometers along the railway, usually in a village or populated area. On orders from the Japanese, the men in charge of these posts were to walk along the rail each morning until they reached

116

the following post. There they were to wait for the morning train. If they didn't want to walk back to their respective posts, they could hitch a ride on the train. When approaching one of these posts, or *ploeg* as they were called, the train's engineer kept his eyes open to see if the track inspector from the following security post had arrived. If he hadn't, the engineer stopped the train or proceeded very slowly because either there was danger on the tracks ahead or something had happened to the inspector.

When the coal line was first set up in Riau, only one man was assigned to inspect each segment of the track. However, not too long afterward, when one of the inspectors was attacked by a tiger on his early morning trek, the Japanese authorities ordered the *lurah* of each of the villages in which a watch post was located to provide a number of local people to accompany the rail inspector on his journey. As it turned out, this order proved to be no hardship and, in fact, became a form of entertainment for people in the isolated villages. Oftentimes as many as ten young men volunteered to walk along with the rail inspector. Interest picked up even more during the fasting month, in mid August, 2605.

Early in the morning on that Thursday a group of about ten voluntary inspectors was heading toward Taratakbuluh from the next whistlestop to the south. The jungle area between that post and the village was known as the tigers' den. It wasn't rare that a pride of tigers would emerge from this den and approach the village. When that happened the people ran for cover, livestock shook in their pens, and dogs scampered beneath houses, their tails between their legs. Locks and bolts in the village clamped shut.

It was fairly bright by the time the railway inspectors from the south approached Taratakbuluh and some of the men had already doused their torches. They joked and told stories, partly to overcome boredom but mostly to overcome fear. The younger ones who had tagged along now had another source of entertainment: stopping atop the trestle, and screaming and throwing their torches out as far as possible over the water. The look of their faces when they did that was one of pure happiness.

Arriving at the other side of the trestle the group sighted a body lying prone on the railroad embankment.

"It's a dead man," one of them said.

"Let's throw him in the river," another suggested.

The official inspector looked at the body more closely.

"He's asleep," the man said.

Two of the walkers nudged the man with their feet.

"Wake up! Wake up!" they shouted at the sleeping man.

Kliwon awoke with a start, surprised to find a crowd of strangers standing around him. He didn't know who they were or why they were here. He had never been out of the camp this early in the morning.

"What do you want?" Kliwon asked the men.

"You're a *romusha*, aren't you?" one of the men stated more than asked.

"Yes," he answered straightforwardly. So what if he was a *romusha*? He had done nothing wrong but he sensed the attitude of the men around him change immediately.

"You were stealing, weren't you?" the men in the group said, almost in unison.

This accusation came as a shock to Kliwon and he jumped to his feet.

"I was not!" he shouted. "Who are you, accusing me of stealing?"

"If you weren't stealing, then what are you doing here so early in the morning?"

This is going too far, Kliwon thought, but knew that he had no chance of taking them on physically. He was greatly outnumbered and would be black and blue even before he had a chance to explain.

"You should watch what you say," he advised them, trying to be patient. "Who are you?" he asked again.

"We're asking the questions!" shouted one of the men in a cocky sort of way. "You are a *romusha* and just finished stealing something. You came here to hide and fell asleep. Isn't that right?"

118

Fear began to overtake Kliwon. His eyes searched for an escape route but none was visible. Should he invite them to Haji Zen's? No. What reason could he give for sleeping on the railroad embankment and not returning to the barracks? How could he keep his face from showing what had actually happened that night? Images of Siti's husband and his friends immediately came to mind.

"I work as a cook at the camp over there," he said.

"You're lying. We're going to take you back to the village and ask people if anything's missing."

"Listen," Kliwon pleaded. "If we go to the village, all they're going to do is send us to see the Japs. We may as well go there directly and get this problem over with."

This suggestion made the men stop to think.

"Come on," Kliwon invited them, aware that he had put them off guard. In a friendly manner he pulled the hand of one of the men and led him back across the bridge. On arriving at the other side Kliwon went down the embankment toward the barracks. The men who had followed stopped. No one wanted to go first.

"Come on," Kliwon called to them.

They said nothing. Feeling greatly relieved, Kliwon turned away from them and continued his walk toward the security post. The group turned around and resumed their walk to Taratakbuluh.

Three soldiers were on guard in the post. "*Ohayo, gozaimas*"—"Good morning"—Kliwon greeted. Only one of the guards took notice. Kliwon went on toward the barracks but stopped first at the makeshift dining table where he opened the bundle he had brought from Haji Zen's house and began to eat the food that was supposed to have been for *sahur.*

The bell had rung eight times by the time Kliwon finished eating but there was no sign that the detainees were to be awaked for work. Kliwon went into the barracks and found the men still asleep, except for Pastor who turned restlessly back and forth on the *balai.* Kliwon felt sorry for the man but he had his own problems to worry about.

The incident on the embankment had upset him. Would those men go around to people's houses? Would they stop at Haji Zen's? If they did, Haji Zen would certainly ask Lena if she had seen him sleeping on the embankment. What answer would she give?

This day should have been the most beautiful day in his life. He should have had the whole day to relive in his mind the night he had spent with the *haji*'s daughter and dream about when he would have the chance to repeat it. Those men on the embankment had hurt his feelings. They had insulted him and spoiled his happiness.

He studied the faces of the Dutch one by one by the daylight that had begun to seep through the cracks in the thatch wall. They hadn't even made a fire for themselves. They must be exhausted. All of them slept soundly, except for Pastor who continued to toss and turn and roll over and back from one side to another.

He must be in great pain, Kliwon thought. Why had Pastor been beaten? Wasn't he the leader of the Dutch? Kliwon attempted to find a link between the man's beating and their escape plans. He could find none. If Lieutenant Ose came back that day, there was hope that the barracks would be completely empty that night.

With a smile of uncertainty on his face, Kliwon fell asleep.

❧

On the second day after the Japanese surrender the people of Pakanbaru were still trying to figure out what had happened. The few available clues were more a source of confusion than help: the Dutch detainees were not being taken out to work; the *Hinomaru* continued to fly in front of offices but had been raised without the customary ceremony; the Japanese were doing their exercises, their *taiso*, in front of their respective offices; guardhouses were still manned but the security post was almost empty; and very few Japanese were about in the city. The most worrisome

120

sign, however, was that the larger stores in town had not opened for trade.

All over the world, merchants and traders serve as primary indicators of social and economic trends. Invariably, they are among the first to react to or first to get wind of new conditions or trends. While the less sensitive are trying to understand what is happening they are already making the necessary preparations or adjustments. Traders have no time to wait because their very fate depends on the strength of their instincts and their ability to take action before conditions change. Now, on the second day after the Japanese surrender, the situation demanded that the traders of Pakanbaru make some decisions.

If peace came, goods that had previously been scarce would begin to flood the market. Absorbing this volume of goods would require money, so money was essential. But what kind of money? Gold? Gold was a good bet but gold coins had vanished from circulation some time ago. Some were in the hands of traders but most had been taken by the Japanese. Shortly after their arrival, the Japanese had ordered that people turn over all gold jewelry and coins bearing the face of a European monarch. These coins would be melted down and new ones of simpler design issued, ones that were more in keeping with the spirit of the Greater East Asian War. Most of the gold that people had managed to hide had been traded for supplies long ago.

And if goods started to flood the market, where would they come from? Java? Singapore? Japan? The United States? Aha!

Before deciding to sell a particular line of goods, a merchant will first find out everything he needs to know about them: where they come from, their volume, availability of production, and so on. Percentage of profit is not necessarily his first consideration because unless he can sell the goods, he is going to go bankrupt. On that Thursday the traders' confusion was compounded by questions of what kind of goods they were to buy, where they were to find them, and what kind of money to use. As a result, many traders sold their stocks only with hesitation. Some raised the price of their goods to twice their normal price; others raised their prices five times over.

Helplessness was on the faces of all the traders. Even so, most were convinced that whatever happened they would make it through safely and, quite possibly, with a profit far greater than they could normally have expected.

Anis shared this belief and knew a true trader would succeed in business even if he had only his muscles to use as starting capital. For that reason, he didn't give much thought that morning to his own business or the air of uncertainty now affecting businesses in town. He focused his attention on the discussion he had had with Agus the night before.

Did he love Lena? To be frank, he didn't even know her. What did Lena have that other girls in the village did not? As far as he knew, Lena was an only child and her father was the richest man in the village. She was pretty, strong, a little proud, and, it appeared, honest and understanding. What were his chances of getting her for his wife? Very great. There didn't seem to be any man in the village whom the family would accept for her husband. His one and only competitor, if he were even that, was a *romusha.* Who wasn't aware of the character of a *romusha?* Didn't all this remind him of Malin Kundang? Possibly, but he would never make the stupid and fatal error that Malin Kundang made. He would not return home.

The six *babelok* headed back toward Simpang Empat Rengkok, the intersection of the road and railway, early in the morning. A coolie pulling a three-wheeled cart followed behind. Along the quiet road they discussed what kind of trade strategy they might adopt in the face of such uncertainty and change. They concluded that the best strategy would be to hold on to their goods, whatever goods they had, even if they were only smoked fish. Smoked fish would keep for a long time, wouldn't it? Besides, fish was an easy commodity to sell. Whatever came to pass, people still had to eat, didn't they? Whether a person called rice, cassava, or sweet potatoes his staple food, smoked fish always made an agreeable side dish.

Anis kept his thoughts to himself during this discussion.

Upon their arrival at the Mangun home, the men in the group quickly informed those who had stayed behind what they had heard or had guessed about the situation as well as their decision not to sell their goods, at least for the time being.

"We came to the same decision," said Sutan Pamenan, the oldest man among them and one of the men who had stayed at the Manguns'.

"I intend to sell my things as soon as possible," Anis announced suddenly. The other traders looked at Anis with disbelief. What did he have up his sleeve? Anis obviously knew something and he was trying to keep it a secret.

"Why?" Sutan Pamenan asked him.

"I'm going to stop trading for a while."

"And save your money? It's not going to be worth the paper it's printed on."

"Why are you so sure of that?"

"With things so uncertain, there's not a trader around who's going to hold on to cash."

"Well, I'm going to do what I want to do."

"Is there something you're not telling us?" Sutan Pamenan asked. The men were growing more and more suspicious.

"No, there isn't. Trust me. I simply want to stop trading for a month or two."

"I'll give you the original price plus cost," Darlis, the youngest among them, said.

Anis looked at Darlis. He had never liked Darlis because the young man reminded him too much of his own brother, Ujang. Ujang had been a great disappointment to him. After finally freeing himself from the hell of forced labor on the construction of the railroad to Sijunjung and getting some financial help from the people of his village who lived

123

in Pakanbaru, there was only one thing he had wanted to do: find Ujang and get his money back so that he could work as a *babelok* again.

It was night when he arrived in Bukittinggi and he went directly to Lower Market and the combination store and home where he and Ujang used to stay overnight. There he learned that Ujang had not returned home as he had been asked to do but had kept up the trade network that Anis had established. According to the landlord, Ujang was due back in Bukittinggi in two or three days' time.

During the two days that Anis waited for Ujang he used up all the money he had with him. When Ujang finally did arrive he showed no sign of emotion whatsoever—not surprise, not happiness either. And he wasn't even thirteen years old!

"Oh, you're back," Ujang said flatly.

That was all. The two brothers didn't even shake hands, much less embrace each other.

Apparently Ujang had learned what had happened to Anis from other Minang men who had escaped from their forced labor before Anis had made his break.

"So, I guess you were able to keep up the business?" Anis said with some pride in his voice because of the success of his younger brother.

"This isn't the same business you left," Ujang informed him.

"What do you mean?"

"I sold the goods you left with me to pay off your debts. I thought you were dead so I turned over the rest of the money to mother. I have a complete ledger. You can ask mother for it tomorrow."

"Is there any money left?"

"I really don't know. I haven't been home in a long time."

"Where did the money come for this, for your business?"

"I earned it myself."

Darlis, the young man standing before him now, resembled Ujang very much. Anis didn't like him but he said nothing about that.

124

"All right, I'll pay you twice the purchase price but not your costs," Darlis said, making a new and apparently final offer.

Anis merely nodded his head. With no formal agreement whatsoever, a quintal of smoked fish had changed hands.

"I'll bring the money to Agus' house this afternoon," Darlis said to Anis later. The tone of his voice was no different from what it would have been in a normal business transaction.

❖

The sound of a large explosion woke up the officers sleeping at the military headquarters. Everyone in the complex was startled and those who ran outside to learn what had happened were quick to find out. The explosion had taken place in the Communications Office where the telephone switchboard that served all of the military posts in Riau was located.

A grenade had destroyed most of the communications equipment and ripped apart the body of the Communications Office commander. According to a sergeant, one of the soldiers assigned to guard the office, Major Yamada, had arrived at the office in drunken condition. After coming in, he ordered them to go back to the barracks to rest. They left but hadn't walked far before the communications office blew up behind them.

There was no apparent panic. Those not immediately concerned shook their heads and returned to bed as if nothing of importance had happened but Ose found himself unable to fall back to sleep.

He lay in bed, observing his colleagues as they dropped off to sleep and then looking at the two school rooms, now one large room. Once, he thought, there would have been about seventy students studying in the two classrooms, children who would grow and become Satiyah, Kliwon, Saleh, Anwar, Ratna . . . the Indonesian people he had come to know so well.

Saleh, or "Sareh-san" as he called him (he had never managed to master the *l* sound), was the principal of the primary school that sat opposite the residency. Saleh, a dark-skinned man, was getting on in years but held the respect of everyone he dealt with. Anwar-san, the young teacher at the primary school, was a bachelor about twenty-five years of age. Ratna-san, the other teacher at the school, was also twenty-five years old. She too was single, an "old maid" as Anwar-san had once joked but with no hint of malice in his voice. Ose had found it difficult to understand why the one teacher should be considered young and the other one old. After all, they were the same age. Ratna-san was a pretty woman but she was strict and was feared by all the students in the school.

Ose was transferred from Singapore to Pakanbaru in early 2603. His friend Shinji—a captain at the time, then a major, and now dead—had been assigned to the Railroad Logistics Division some time before. Apparently, Shinji had played some kind of role in his transfer but he didn't know at the time whether to be thankful or not. Without any clear roster of duties Ose wasn't even sure why he was in Pakanbaru. Each morning he would ride his bicycle to the office of the commander in chief of the Riau Regional Military Command. After reporting in, he would chat with other officers who had nothing to do. Then he would go for a ride around town on his bicycle, while away his time at the *warung* in front of the primary school, or simply go home and sleep.

Ose wasn't happy with the situation and put in a request to be seconded to the city's school system. He insisted that there was much he could do and his request was soon granted.

At the outset of his work at the two primary schools in Pakanbaru, Ose had certain hours to keep in each. His heart, however, remained fixed in Primary One, the school opposite the residency where Sareh-san, Anwar-san, and Ratna-san worked. As time went by Ose's respect for Sareh-san grew and he came to enjoy a close friendship with the two young teachers. Anwar-san came to his place four or five times a week to teach him Bahasa Indonesia, and at school the three of them worked hard to teach the young children Japanese folk songs and marching tunes. Ose also helped teach sports and *sumo* came to be one of the students' favorite subjects.

Where are they now? Ose wondered. It was too bad that it was fasting month and the schools were closed. If not, he could have gone to Primary One to tell his friends about Japan's defeat. As friends, the news should be given to them personally.

"Do you still remember my friend, Chiuko? She's the lucky one! Her husband lost a foot in Saipan and is now in Tokyo working at the War Ministry. Chiuko's invited me to visit and I think I'll take her up on the invitation. Maybe through her husband I will be able to work out a better way of getting mail to you." Ose thought over the last letter he had received from Michiko. That had been last year, sometime around the middle of the year. Now he could only shrug his shoulders. He didn't particularly like what had happened but there was nothing he could do now to change it. He thought it so strange that his wife had wanted him to be a hero.

After reading the letter, he had put it out of his mind because he was busy with Ratna-san directing the students in a performance that was scheduled for the end of the school year. The performance proved to be a great success. The commander in chief himself had attended and smiled with satisfaction upon seeing the children singing and dancing to Japanese songs. He must have been thinking of his own children at the time.

The people most satisfied with the performance were Ose and his friends. In the following year, when he was rehearsing the school's end-of-the-year performance, he had received his orders for transfer to Taratakbuluh. Nonetheless he made a special trip back to Pakanbaru to attend.

In early 2605 Ose received a letter from his father. His father's greetings for a happy new year were customary ones but, at the same time, somewhat strange because his father had never written him before. Recalling its contents, Ose was surprised that the letter had been able to slip by the censor's usually ready hands: "Your children are with me now. Your mother and your sisters enjoy them and think of them as replacements for you. Michiko did not return from Tokyo. Last month your sisters went there in hopes of finding her and bringing her home. They found her but she is the mistress of a general in the War Ministry. Consider her dead. I told the boys that their mother is dead and we placed a plaque with her name on the family altar. That way they'll have a mother they can continue to honor and respect. We've been having to go to the bomb shelter every day for a month now because of air attacks by the Allied forces. We might have to evacuate the city soon."

"Can you read *kanji?*" Ose asked Anwar-san in Japanese one evening when the young teacher was giving him a Bahasa Indonesia lesson. In fact, he need not have asked. He knew that while Anwar-san was fairly fluent in spoken Japanese and was able to read *katagana* and *hiragana*, he knew only a few *kanji.*

"*Sukoshi,* a little," the teacher answered.

"Try reading this," Ose said.

Anwar took the letter from Ose's hands, scanned it, and then handed it back.

"It's much too difficult for me," Anwar said in Japanese.

"The letter is from my father," Ose informed him. "He said my wife has gone off with another man. A general."

"What did you say? I don't understand?" Anwar told him.

Ose repeated what he had said in Indonesian. The young teacher's mouth dropped open. His face lost its color and lines appeared on his forehead. Ose could see that Anwar's seriousness was not feigned.

Ose laughed at the sight of his friend. "Why are you so sad? Who is it that lost his wife? You or I?" he asked in Japanese.

Anwar seemed not to comprehend what he had said and Ose repeated himself in Indonesian. Thereafter they spoke only in Indonesian.

"But you love your wife, Ose-san," Anwar said as he pointed to the picture of Ose's wife on the small bureau.

Ose took the picture and placed it face downward.

"No, she's not right for me any more. My poor kids. They're with my father now."

"You can marry again. You can look for someone who is right for you," Anwar said. The young teacher laughed and Ose laughed with him.

"Do you have any candidates?"

"Ratna-san!"

Ose laughed louder.

"Of course. Ratna-san," the teacher said again. "You two know how to work together. I'm sure she would be willing."

"Me marry an old maid?" Ose asked, still laughing.

The two men laughed together.

Ose felt empty inside and his laughter did little to fill the vacuum. In fact, it made him feel even more miserable and seemed to accentuate the loss he felt. Nonetheless, he was moved by the young man's sympathy and his attempt to cheer him. If only Anwar-san could read *kanji*, he thought. He would appreciate his father's letter with its straightforward and simple style.

The commotion that arose in the complex after Major Yamada blew himself up with a grenade seemed to have taken place ages ago. Ose now listened to the sounds of the military headquarters beginning to wake. Today, for the first time, headquarters was the home of a defeated army.

Ose didn't wish to return to Taratakbuluh immediately. He wanted to look around the city, to speak with colleagues, and, if there were still time, to see friends after he paid his last respects to Major Shinji, the man who had been his friend, his brother-in-law, and his guardian.

The other officers seemed to be of the same mind and were in no rush to take the morning train back to their respective camps.

❀

It was nine o'clock in the morning Tokyo time. Kiguchi awaked and, stretching as he moved, went to the security post. The soldiers on guard greeted him and cleared a place on the bench for him to sit down. He picked up the telephone receiver to call Pakanbaru. The phone was out of order.

"Out of order again," he muttered in complaint.

The rest of the soldiers woke up, came into the security post, said good morning, and went directly to the river.

"Wake the Dutch up," Kiguchi ordered the two soldiers who were on guard.

The soldiers went to the barracks where they began to hit its thatch walls with the butts of their rifles while shouting "Wake up! Wake up!" in Bahasa Indonesia.

Rudely awakened from their sleep, the Dutch began to swear but nonetheless made haste to leave. Pastor alone remained on the *balai* pretending to be asleep. No one paid any attention to him, not even Kliwon.

What have I done wrong? Pastor asked himself. Would his boycott raise sympathy for him and foster among the detainees a feeling of solidarity? If he could succeed in that and if the men were to follow his example he might be able to join them in their escape without too much loss of face. What had ever made them side with Wimpie?

The detainees were relieved when they were not immediately ordered to line up for roll call and then even more so when Freddie was told to serve them breakfast. They had never before been allowed to have breakfast. While waiting for breakfast to be cooked, they sat around their makeshift dining table. "I think I'll go along with you," a former supporter of Pastor said to Wimpie.

"Me too," said another.

"Me too."

"Me too."

Pastor had no more followers left. Not a single man wanted to stay behind with him in detention. Pastor was despondent; he had heard the whole conversation.

Although extremely happy, Wimpie chose not to laugh or show his delight. He remained where he was and stared at the men, one by one. Such a look of seriousness marked their faces. He was pleased by what he saw but also aware of the increased responsibility that had just been placed on his shoulders. He had hoped that the men would recognize him as their leader but had never actually expected it to happen and certainly not so quickly as this. He had always had to be on guard, always afraid that someone would try to usurp his power. But not now. Slowly, a sense of calm began to seep into his consciousness.

Finally, he spoke. "I'm glad you're going with me. The more the better, I say. I hope Pastor will change his mind and come along."

Kliwon didn't understand what was happening but didn't worry about it either. He had his own problems to worry about. While the other men were eating, Kliwon, for lack of anything to do, took a bowl of rice porridge to Pastor.

"Eat up, Pastor," he said.

The man to whom he spoke said nothing. He remained motionless, pretending to be asleep. Kliwon knew the man was only pretending and he continued trying to get the man to eat. After a time, however, he gave up and retreated outside with the bowl. All the Dutch around the table outside turned toward him and stared.

The detainees were still eating when ten bells sounded. Kiguchi walked over and stood atop the makeshift podium used for roll calls. Noticing the sergeant, the Dutch stiffened. Although still weak and tired, they gulped down what food was left in their bowls and ran to fall into the line forming in front of Sergeant Kiguchi.

Roll call began. One of the soldiers was sent to the barracks to find Pastor but was almost knocked over when the man he was looking for came out of the barracks at the same time that he was going in.

Immediately after falling into line, Pastor raised his arm and screamed at the sergeant in Indonesian: "This is impermissible, Masta! Do you people have no sense of humanitarianism at all?"

Wimpie shouted at Pastor in Dutch: "Van Roscott! What are you trying to prove? You've said enough!"

"Yes, Pastor," another man added. "Do what the Jap says or you're going to be beaten up again."

Pastor ignored the other men and with his fist still in the air approached Sergeant Kiguchi and shouted: "You are animals! You show no regard for regulations! You flout the rules of the Geneva convention . . ."

"Watch it, Pastor, he's going to hit you."

One after the other, Sergeant Kiguchi's fists flew out at Pastor, hitting him squarely in the face. The Dutchman reeled. Still not satisfied, Kiguchi stepped down from the podium, raised Pastor with one arm, and threw him back to the ground.

The rest of the Dutch were ordered to begin work. This left Pastor alone screaming and shouting in place. The man could barely stand.

"Gag him!" Kiguchi shouted to one of the soldiers.

The soldier took a small towel and putting it over Pastor's mouth wrapped it around his head and knotted it in the back. Pastor still tried to scream.

Another soldier took a piece of rope and, pushing Pastor against a rubber tree, pulled his arms back and tied them together behind the tree. Not even waiting for orders from Kiguchi, the soldiers took turns slapping Pastor in the face but soon they tired of this.

After the soldiers stopped hitting him, Pastor slumped into a sitting position and with his hands still tied behind the tree fell unconscious.

Satiyah watched what was happening outside from the cracks in the thatch wall of her hut. Her stomach churned with disgust. She had seen the Japanese torture numerous people and every time it was different. And every time she watched she said to herself this is how Mas Alimin must have been tortured. This is how he must have felt. Or maybe even worse. If not, he wouldn't have come home in the condition he did.

In mid August, 2602, two weeks after her husband had left for the training course, Satiyah bore her third child. Although she sent messages to inform him, he didn't come home as he had promised. Satiyah's father himself made the trip to Semarang to convey the happy news but all he brought back was a short letter from her husband, expressing his happiness at the birth of their child but explaining that he was unable to take time off from his important work for the prosperity of Greater East Asia.

Mas Alimin didn't even come home for Lebaran which that year fell during the second week of October. In fact, he didn't come home until late October after the course had officially ended. He returned to Mersi thin, pale, and feverish.

The catastrophe began that night. They were unclothed and in bed and Satiyah embraced her husband expecting to rouse in him the passion that she herself was feeling. But he did nothing. She waited and waited but her husband could do nothing at all.

Finding himself unable to make love Alimin threw himself on the mattress and began to cry uncontrollably. Not really understanding what was happening, Satiyah too began to cry. She nestled against her husband, pressing her body against his back.

"Shh, shh, there now," she said soothingly. "You're tired. You haven't been eating well. You'll be all right soon. You'll see."

Her words did nothing to stop his tears.

"Hush, hush, You'll wake the children."

Alimin did not regain his sexual power and gradually this began to create tension in the household. Then their third child died, the one who had been born while Ndoro Alimin was attending the training course, and the sadness in their home increased. Eventually, Satiyah learned to cope with the strain and live with her husband's silence and lack of attention to her needs.

In March, 2603, a huge celebration was held in Purwokerto to commemorate the first anniversary of the coming of the Japanese to Java. The teachers and all the students from the town's junior and senior high schools were brought to the *alun-alun*, the town park and plaza, where the festivities were centered. Satiyah took her two children and watched the celebration from the edge of the park.

"Papa! Papa!" the two boys shouted upon seeing their father lead his students into the park.

"Is your husband a teacher?"

Satiyah turned toward the voice and saw a woman slightly older than herself standing not too far away. She too had children with her.

"Yes, he is," Satiyah answered politely.

"This is a coincidence. My husband is a teacher, too. He's the one over there, the one with no hair."

"Mine doesn't have any hair either. Not since he returned from that intensive Japanese course in Semarang."

"He was there too? Which group was he in?"

"The first one, the one that was held during Ramadan."

"What is your husband's name?"

"Alimin."

"Oh . . ."

"Do you know him?"

"My husband does. He's mentioned his name often."

"Alimin never talks about his friends."

"Where is the baby who was born when he was away?"

"She died."

"Oh, my God, I'm sorry. First your husband's beaten half to death and then the baby . . ."

Satiyah stepped back in surprise. It had never occurred to her that her kind and likable husband might have been beaten.

"You mean, he didn't tell you about it?" the woman asked.

Satiyah shook her head, unable to speak. The tears that suddenly welled in her eyes began to run down her cheeks.

"It's because he demanded to go home that they beat him. Then for the same reason, they wouldn't let him come home for Lebaran either. He asked my husband to visit you but I guess he never got around to it."

That evening when her husband came home from the celebration and parade Satiyah knelt beside the chair in which he sat and put her arms around his legs. Still sweating and breathing hard, Alimin looked exhausted.

134

"They beat you. The Japanese beat you, didn't they?" Satiyah screamed.

Her husband said nothing. Satiyah wanted to ask him why he hadn't told her and why he hadn't allowed her to share his suffering but, maybe because of his silence, didn't. Alimin stroked Satiyah's hair and then with difficulty stood up and released himself from his wife's embrace.

"I'm going to take a bath," he said. Satiyah could do nothing but let him go.

It was eleven o'clock. The morning train from Pakanbaru would arrive shortly. Kiguchi ordered van Roscott to be taken back into the barracks. Two of the soldiers unbound the rope that held his hands together and the towel that was wrapped around his head. They then dragged the man to the barracks.

Somewhere between consciousness and unconsciousness Pastor still found the power to mumble, "God *Verdomme!* You are animals!"

❁

The sun was high before Lena awoke. Because she hadn't been awaked, she had missed *subuh* prayers. Haji Zen had always been strict with his other children but with Lena it was somewhat different. After all, she was the baby of the family, wasn't she?

"It's a sin for you to treat the children differently. You're not setting a proper example for her," Haji Deramah often complained when she felt that Lena deserved some kind of warning or punishment which her husband had failed to give.

"We have spent our entire life in prayer and devotion," Haji Zen replied. "Maybe a little sin is not so bad," he joked. "That way we'll have some idea of what it is they call hell."

It was the strident sound of her father's voice that woke Lena up that morning. Her father was in the front room and

Lena, in her bedroom, was able to hear quite clearly everything that he said.

"Well then you must have two bodies. I could swear I saw you walking on the path behind the mosque yesterday evening. But you said you were at the crossing until late at night!"

Lena heard Paktua Hasan laugh. "Maybe you were just seeing things," he said.

"Why should I be seeing things?" Haji Zen said in return. "Weren't you afraid waiting there in the jungle by yourself?" he then asked.

"A little. But if you're afraid of danger, then it doesn't matter where you are. You're still going to be afraid."

"But alone in the jungle at night! I call that looking for danger."

"No, it's not. Not if you're there for a good reason. Don't worry about me. If my time's not come I'm not about to die."

Haji Zen burst into laughter. "You drag that knife of yours across your neck and say: 'My time's not come so I'm not going to die.' We'll see whether you die or not."

"Well, if I died then I guess my time would have come." Now it was Paktua Hasan who laughed.

A moment later the tone of the men's voices grew more serious.

"Fact of the matter is, I wanted to talk to you yesterday about Kliwon," Paktua Hasan said to Haji Zen.

"What about Kliwon?" Haji Zen's voice had regained the tone of authority that caused people in the village to respect him. All traces of humor were gone.

"I don't think he should go along."

"But he told me that it would be dangerous for him to stay here. He said that the Japanese would beat him and torture everyone in the village if they found out he was hiding here."

"I don't know about that. It's just that I've got a bad feeling."

Lena's blood coursed through her veins. Did Paktua Hasan know what had happened last night?

"What do you mean by 'a bad feeling'?"

"I don't really know. I just feel like something is going to go wrong."

"You mean something is going to happen to Kliwon?"

"I don't know. It's not all that clear."

"Well, what exactly is it you fear?"

"I feel that someone, that more than one person is going to die."

"But you don't really believe that, do you? That's prophesying, which is just as bad as belief in more than one god. It's *syirik*, the only sin that God will not forgive."

"I couldn't tell you whether it's *syirik* or not, but I know what my heart is telling me. I have a bad feeling so I think it would be best if Kliwon didn't go along. If it's only the Dutch who are with me I'll have more leeway, more freedom to act."

"I leave it up to you, Hasan," Haji Zen said after a few moments. "The only problem now is what to do about tonight. We have a visitor coming and for this visitor at least it would be best if Kliwon weren't here."

Surprised, anxious, and upset, Lena felt a mixture of emotions upon hearing this.

"May I know who the visitor is?" Paktua Hasan asked Haji Zen.

"No reason why not. He's one of the Minang traders who stays at Haji Usman's on market days."

"Does he intend to ask you for your daughter?"

"It would seem that way but I've made no promises."

It wasn't until long after Paktua Hasan left that Lena finally emerged from the bedroom. She pretended to have just awaked.

"You weren't up for prayers this morning," her mother scolded.

"Well, why didn't anyone wake me up?" Lena asked and went directly into the bath.

137

By the time Lena had finished bathing it was almost midday. As quietly as possible, she collected a few articles of clothing and wrapped them in a blanket. She then went to find her mother who was in the kitchen, beginning to cook.

"I'm going to Jamilah's house," she told her mother.

"What is happening at Jamilah's?"

"They're making rice flour."

"Rice flour? Only a week into the fasting month and they're already making rice flour? I'm the one who needs the help. We're having guests this evening."

"Who's coming?"

"I don't know. Friends of your father, I guess."

"How many?"

"Two, maybe three."

"Well, if it's only three people you won't need my help," Lena said in her pampered way. "That should be nothing for you."

"Well, don't be too late. What's that you have with you?"

"My sarong and prayer veil," Lena answered.

Jamilah's home was located at the edge fo the village, about four hundred meters from the bank of the river. Lena set off in the direction of her friend's home but upon arrival there, instead of going into the house she turned onto the footpath that led upriver. During the fasting month, especially when it coincides with the dry season, few people leave their homes during the day. Most people stay inside their homes or in the mosque, sitting, dozing, or waiting in the shade until evening or time for prayer. No one but Lena was on the path.

After a half hour of walking Lena came to one of the many branches of the network of rivers and swamps in the Kampar Kanan basin. After the death of the area's rubber trade, fishing had become the primary livelihood of many people in the area, and the spot where Lena now stood was one of the numerous trapping sites. A number of *perahu* were on the river bank but Lena could see no one around. She chose for herself one of the smaller boats, took a paddle, and began to make her way upstream.

138

During the dry season the rivers recede and the shallow bed becomes calm and clear. The branch of the river that Lena now plied was only three to five meters wide and almost completely covered over by the thick foliage of rubber trees that lined its banks. Lena paddled effortlessly, apparently unaware of the look of desperate confusion on her face.

Why was she doing this? she wondered. Running away was completely unnecessary. Had she been frank with her parents and told them what she and Kliwon had done, her father would have summoned Kliwon immediately and had them married that very same night. But what her father had done was too much. He had allowed another man to propose to her! He deserved a little punishment.

After an hour of paddling in and out through the jungle Lena arrived at the Kampar Kanan River. Rubber trees were replaced by reeds and soon, a few meters ahead, the large river stretched out in front of her. She paddled across the river and, upon reaching the other side, turned the boat upstream. She then began to skirt the river bank, entering each and every inlet she passed in search of Paktua Hasan's boat. It wasn't too long before she found it. The boat had been dragged up on shore, turned over, and tied to a rubber tree.

Lena hugged the bank of the river with her boat, then stepped ashore and dragged the boat as far as possible out of the water. After tethering the boat and turning it over, she took her bundle and began following the soft, green moss-covered path that ran beneath the shade of the rubber trees toward the crossing point.

❁

"I worry about you," Agus said to Anis after being told that Anis had sold all his stock to Darlis. "I wouldn't want to see your chickens scatter before you have any more eggs to hatch."

"Neither would I, but it's a risk I have to take. If I've made the wrong choice, so be it. When I first started in business, all I had for capital were these bones of mine and nothing more. If need be, I can start from nothing once more."

"I just don't want you to get your hopes up too high."

"But if I don't try, I will never know my chances of success."

"Are you taking the evening train?" Mar asked.

"Yes," Anis answered.

After leaving Agus' place, Anis went to Sutan Mudo's store which doubled as a bus terminal for passengers going to Bukittinggi. During the past month Sutan Mudo had purchased all the smoked fish the traders brought to town.

"Go ahead, keep those fish of yours," Sutan Mudo said to Anis as he entered the store. "For you it's going to be like falling off a ladder and then having the ladder come falling down on top of you. With the war over, the price of goods is going to fall and those fish of yours are going to rot."

"Sutan Mudo! What are you so fired up about?" Anis asked while laughing at the man. Although Anis never took the liberty of dropping *Sutan,* a fairly formal term of address, when speaking to his friend, their relationship was nonetheless a close one. Somewhat odd, too, was the way Anis addressed Agus. With Agus, Anis always spoke in the familiar, never using the term of address *Kakak* or "Older Brother," the salutation customarily used by a person his age when speaking with an older male, especially one who is married. But here again, their relationship was a special one and laxity in prescribed behavior caused no problem.

"I'm not fired up. Why would I be fired up? But you guys are too much. One day you don't see the Dutch let out of their cages and you start holding your goods. Do you think I'm going to starve because you won't sell me your fish?"

"Calm down or you're going to turn your hair gray. Besides, it's fasting month and you lose any merit you've gained if you get angry." Anis continued to laugh.

"You just keep in mind that when you want to sell I might not want to buy. So there!"

"I've already sold my goods."

"Who to?"

"Darlis. He paid me twice the purchase price."

140

"He's crazy. Does he think prices are going to double? Where did he steal the money to buy your stuff?"

"I don't know. You'll have to ask him."

"Ach! Kids today. Just because you can count on your fingers doesn't mean you're so smart."

Neither of the two men spoke for a while.

"What is going on around here?" Anis then asked in a more serious voice.

"No one seems to know for sure," Sutan Mudo answered. "No radio, no newspapers, not even an announcement from the government. Who could possibly know what's going on?"

"Why are the stores closed?"

"Because people think the war is over."

"Why? Because the Dutch weren't taken out to work?"

"That plus the fact the Japanese haven't been showing their faces either."

"And what do you think?"

Sutan Mudo paused before answering. He spoke slowly.

"It looks like the Japanese lost."

"Is that possible?"

"Seems like it. They're paying for their sins. Besides, Japan's alone now and has lots of enemies."

"What about Japanese money? All my savings are in Japanese money."

"I'm worried about that too. I don't know where to get rid of it. I sent Sudin, my wife's brother, down to Lower Market to buy up all the nonperishables he can find but I don't know how much luck he's going to have because everyone else is doing the same thing."

"If that's the case then villages might be the best bet."

"I have lots of cash, but what's there to buy in the villages? The people there don't have anything left to sell."

"I'm going to Taratakbuluh tonight," Anis said carefully.

"Do they have any smoked fish there?"

"They wouldn't right now. They're probably catching them or smoking them but I might be able to get a guarantee of purchase with a down payment."

"How much fish does that place produce in a week?"

"Six or seven quintals."

"Then take my money and buy them all."

"How am I supposed to do that?"

"I don't know. Just take the money. I trust you with it. Buy at any price and we'll split the profits fifty-fifty."

"Why don't you come with me?"

"I can't. I'll send Sudin with you but I want you to hold onto the money. He's a bit slow in the head."

"I'd prefer to have you come along. We could go to Sungai Pagar tomorrow. There should be a ton or more of smoked fish at the market on Saturday."

"What do you need me for? Sudin will be with you. Besides, if I weren't along you'd have much more freedom."

"But the problem is I actually want you along for something else. I need your help."

"Well, tell me what it is and I'll consider it."

"I'm intending to propose to the daughter of a *haji* in Taratakbuluh. I promised that I would be back this evening with my 'older brother' but Agus won't go with me."

"So that's why you got rid of your things so fast."

"Yes."

"Why do you want to marry someone from around here? Aren't there any girls left in your village?"

"But if the girl you want to marry is from somewhere else what are you supposed to do?"

"Is her father well off?"

"Yes, the richest man in the village. His rubber estate is . . ."

"Rubber?" Sutan Mudo asked, cutting Anis off in mid-sentence.

"Yes, rubber."

"If the war is over, that means the rubber market will come back to life."

"Could be, but I haven't had time to think about that."

"I'm going with you. What time do we leave?"

It was still early, only twelve o'clock Tokyo time, so Anis spent his time walking around the town and through Lower Market. Most of the stores were open. Only the large stores, the ones selling household goods and hardware, were closed. The small shops, the food stores, and the eating stalls were open and operating as usual. People selling kitchen supplies were doing a brisk business. Meat and fish were still available.

If Sutan Mudo wants to exchange his money for goods, he could buy meat, Anis thought. Meat and fish can be dried and stored. But there wasn't all that much for sale and people like Sutan Mudo didn't concern themselves with small trade. Their minds were on big operations: on big stores closing their doors, on tons of smoked fish, or on huge profits from rejuvenation of the rubber market. They concerned themselves only with truly profitable investments; small-time trade wasn't worth the bother.

Clusters of people were everywhere, in the market and in the streets, and were invariably circled by children and young people who were out of school and hoping to hear what was being said. Groups of people stood along the side of the road. Groups sat in food stalls (which were open though not selling food because of the fasting month). Clusters of men gathered at the docks on the chocolate-colored waters of the Siak River.

Was this the end of the war? It was so quiet, so placid, so inconspicuous an end. The war itself had never come to this place. The area had seen no air war, no bombings and strafings, or the slaughter of civilians that was said to have taken place so frequently during this war. The town had been a haven, but now that the war was over there seemed to be something missing. Something had gone and left behind an emptiness and uncertain yearning.

Pakanbaru had always been a peaceful place. The coming of the Japanese and then the Dutch and the *romusha* caused some problems, as did the scarcity of food staples and other supplies, but these had not been insurmountable. Even the sense of involvement that later arose, the feeling of being involved in a huge and horrible war whose goals were beyond an ordinary man's comprehension. That too had never in fact seemed real.

Now it appeared the war was over and whatever sense of involvement had once existed, suddenly faded. Whatever people felt about the war, whether they approved or disapproved was no longer important. Its end had created an entirely new situation. People no longer knew where they stood or where they were to go. Revenge, suffering, sacrifice were suddenly matters of no consequence. Their importance had vanished as quickly as a nightmare after waking.

This is now what everyone discussed.

❧

"I didn't think you were coming," Haji Usman said upon the arrival of Anis and Sutan Mudo in Taratakbuluh that evening. "I was getting nervous."

Six bells, the signal that it was six o'clock Tokyo time, had sounded some time before. Anis introduced Sutan Mudo as a distant relative and presented Haji Usman with a small gift which he graciously accepted.

"One should always try to keep his promises," Anis said. What he didn't add was, "Even when their relevance seems to have vanished."

"I don't know what I would have done if you hadn't come. I spoke again with Haji Zen at *lohor* and would have been embarrassed to tell him now you couldn't come."

"Has anything happened since I left?"

"Not really. Just that the *romusha* wasn't able to run away. The Dutch prisoners were forced to work all last night."

Anis thought this matter over. Thousands of possible responses came to mind but in the end he was forced to dismiss them. It would be best not to say anything at all about last night's happenings.

After *asar* prayers, Sutan Mudo began to talk.

"Do the smoked fish the *babelok* sell in Pakanbaru come from the river here?" he asked Haji Usman, pretending not to know.

"Some, but most come from the river's branches and from swamps in the area."

144

"So, on a given day, most of the people here are off catching fish?"

"Yes, I guess so," Haji Usman answered, showing little interest in continuing this line of conversation.

"Where do they smoke the fish?" Sutan Mudo asked.

"Wherever they're caught."

"Do the fishermen live there too?"

"No. They have huts there, but don't live in them. They're used by those whose turn it is to watch the traps."

"But the people wait until market day to sell their fish?"

"That's right."

"Why don't you buy them up beforehand?"

"With what?" Haji Usman answered, still showing no interest.

"I could provide the capital. You could get a lien on the fish with a down payment. I'd take them off your hands and give you part of the profits."

This offer did the trick. Haji Usman suddenly livened up and began to show some interest. Anis watched as the two men made plans and Sutan Mudo handed over to Haji Usman a sum of money.

❧

The war was over. No, that was wrong. Japan had surrendered and now it seemed the time had come to make an accounting of the gains and losses of this war. Overall, the Japanese had clearly suffered a loss. Hundreds of thousands of their best sons had been sacrificed. The country had been destroyed. People who had escaped death now lived in physical and spiritual suffering. The greatest suffering of all appeared to have its source in the uncertainty of the future and regret for the past.

Were there any gains? What was the value of the lesson that force yields little fruit? The future would tell. If the survivors of this war did not mature and did not learn to accept that simple truth, then the war had produced no gains whatsoever. It had been a complete loss.

For Ose, it wasn't the war that had taught him this lesson. He had learned it in childhood. He had known it even then. No, the war had taught him nothing.

Michiko had left him. In one way Ose considered this a gain. It was better to be separated than living together, each one with a disparate set of values and norms, especially now after what she had done.

His children were at their grandfather's. That too was a gain. If nothing else, his parents were good and honest people with the ability to accept things for what they were. He prayed that the American bombs had spared them. If his sons were alive and safe and had not suffered too much from their evacuation and loss of food, the experience could very well shape them into strong and upright adults.

The bundle of jewelry and Satiyah: what was he to do with these gifts from Shinji? Of what real value were they to him? Would they gain him anything? If he were to become a prisoner of war he couldn't be sure of even keeping his life. But then, it was not certain that the Americans would be as cruel as the Japanese had been to the Dutch detainees.

What about the Dutch internees under his authority? They too were in his thoughts. Could he say to them, "I have treated you well and now it is your responsibility to see that I am justly treated by the victors of this war"? Ose felt ashamed for even asking himself such a question and hastily put it out of his mind.

The train moved slowly, averaging no more than thirty kilometers per hour. Downhill it moved faster but uphill it slowed to a crawl. The locomotive would snort and wheeze and sometimes stop altogether. They weren't even as far as Rengkok yet it was there that the real climb began. Getting stuck there was nothing out of the ordinary. The train would roll back down the incline until it came to a stop by itself. The cars would be braked and the train would remain motionless until the locomotive had built up enough steam, 12 on the gauge, to attempt the incline once more.

How was he to convey the news to the detainees? How would they react? Would Wimpie still try to take revenge?

146

He could remember clearly what had happened. Would Wimpie have forgotten?

Ose hadn't paid too much attention to the tension building among the detainees. The underwater work on the trestle supports was finished. Dem had played an important role in seeing that the work was done properly and now, it seemed, was vying with Wimpie to become the unofficial leader of the group. Even then their influence over the men had far offset that of Pastor van Roscott, the group's official leader, who had been appointed by the Japanese.

Wimpie, the unofficial leader, made his presence known everywhere and few were willing to dispute his position. Accidents befell those who did. A man might be crushed by a falling rail, slip off the embankment, become mired in the swamp, or fall from a moving train. Wimpie had so much sway among some of the men that they massaged his feet for him in the evening and brought him his food. Wimpie had rights over the largest portion of food, the best bed, the easiest work.

Ose got the feeling that Dem had been pushed into conflict with Wimpie. Dem, a former member of the Dutch Olympic swim team, was a muscular man who resembled Johnny Weissmuller, the film star, but was a soft-spoken and stubborn man as well. He also must have been a little stupid, a little naïve, Ose thought, to have allowed himself to be pushed up against Wimpie, the notoriously brutal boxer.

The inevitable conflict occurred and Dem, albeit strong, was beaten half to death. Wimpie pounded his fists into Dem's face so fast and so hard that Dem had little choice but to fall back and try to protect his face and body while looking for an opportunity to take a swing at Wimpie. Even though Dem's attempts to defend himself had in the end proved ineffectual, he must have been very strong. Blood poured from his face and though he continued to fall he always got back on his feet again.

It was then that Ose appeared. He grabbed Wimpie's right arm at the wrist and pressed his right hand into Wimpie's chest as a sign for him to fall back. Stunned for a moment, Wimpie then swung his right fist toward Ose's face. Ose was faster. With a light parry, a twist and a throw, the much larger Dutchman went tumbling through the air and landed face downward on the ground with his right arm still in the air behind him in Ose's left hand.

Wimpie fell very hard but didn't sprain his arm. Pain and surprise showed on his face. And then a great deal of fear as well, for he suddenly realized that Ose could have killed him with no effort whatsoever and without having to worry that the incident would ever be investigated.

Wimpie looked as if he were going to bow and ask for forgiveness, but Ose didn't allow this to happen. "Work!" he screamed and all the Dutch went hurrying back to their work.

Two days later Dem was killed in an accident.

That was a month ago. Now, what was going to happen today?

The train moved slowly forward, twisting, turning, climbing, and descending through the jungled heart of Sumatra. The locomotive groaned and every once in a while stopped to build up steam for a climb or to pick up people in need of a ride. The jungle panorama receded—its stands of soaring trees, dense underbrush, swamps wth their chocolate-colored water, mountains, gorges, and streams.

The sun had completed nearly three quarters of its daily journey. The wind had died, leaving the branches of the trees hardly moving at all. It was so strange, Ose thought. Even in the middle of the dry season and even with no clouds to block the glare of the sun, the air in this country never felt really hot. The leaves were perpetually green. Thousands of animals inhabited this jungle; they merely disappeared when the sound of the train went past. After the train passed, jungle life returned to normal. Static. Relaxed. The provident jungle fulfilled the needs of its inhabitants and followed only one law: the weak, whose fate it was to become food for the strong, bred at a faster rate and produced more offspring than the strong while the strong took only what they needed for the day.

Were the Dutch planning to run away into the jungle? And follow the jungle's rules? If so, they would not come out of it safely.

What was he to say to his men, his ten *heitei-san,* upon his return to Taratakbuluh?

Sergeant Kiguchi's attitude seemed to be the proper one: being a Dai Nippon soldier, to act in the manner that is customary for Japanese soldiers. At the very least, this freed one from problematic moral considerations. Then too, in the case of defeat, this provided an easy way for the victors to mete a just and equitable sentence.

Supposing that he had entrusted authority for the order of his small camp to Kiguchi some time before, his life in the camp would have been a much more enjoyable one and his only choice now would be *hara-kiri.*

What had Shinji been thinking about when he pressed the point of his bayonet to his chest and began pulling it toward his heart? Ose had been wrong. Shinji had not killed himself with a pistol. In the last remaining moments of his life he had become a *samurai* once more and ended his life in the manner prescribed by ancient tradition. Even so, what had he been thinking about at the time?

The train stopped in Taratakbuluh and Ose jumped off without a look back at the other commanders on the train. There had been little talk among them since the previous day. They had acted in zombie-like fashion: waking in the morning, eating, sitting, thinking, attending the final ceremonies for those who had committed *hara-kiri,* returning to the dormitory, eating lunch, walking to Rintis Station, boarding the first car they came to, sitting, thinking again. Were the others thinking of *hara-kiri* too?

Ose waited for the train to leave. At the camp the Dutch were working, as usual, in orderly fashion, just as was demanded by the three soldiers watching them.

The soldiers saluted when Ose approached.

Ose came closer and shouted, "Take them to their barracks now!"

❖

Except for a number of small and fairly unimportant differences, Satiyah found her life in Taratakbuluh with Ose very much like her life in Mersi with Ndoro Alimin prior to the time of their catastrophe. Life in Taratakbuluh was calm. This had been almost completely unexpected. She always knew what Ose wanted and Ose, for his part, always exhibited a feeling of understanding.

Only once had she had to go shopping without money from Ose and the money she had used had immediately been replaced. At night she was able to sleep in peace without worrying or wondering whether somethng might happen, something now she even half longed for. But that was not important. A peaceful life was far more important than one of passion and sexual satisfaction. Hadn't she been able to do without it when Ndoro Alimin lost his sexual power? Even with Misran, she had done it only to assure the security of her life with Alimin, her beloved husband. That she had later come to enjoy her relationship with Misran was a sin. She recognized that but felt that by now she had paid sufficient retribution. Ndoro Alimin should be satisfied with the punishment and the suffering she had been forced to bear. Perhaps it was he who had intervened and brought her to Taratakbuluh for this peaceful life with Ose. Perhaps not. Perhaps this was only one more part of his ongoing curse.

During the past couple of days Ose had done little more than sit and think. His manner reminded Satiyah of a time of fear and unrest that she would have preferred to forget. Fortunately, Ose was eating (though not very much), and he drank, bathed, changed his clothes, and had even taken a trip. When Ose was engaged in everyday activities Satiyah's heart beat in normal time but when he stopped working or started to think, her heart raced out of control. Had she done something wrong? Or was this part of Alimin's curse?

150

Her unending feelings of guilt. Was she to lose her kind and gentle Masta too?

That Thursday seemed to pass slowly, far slower than all the other days she had spent in Taratakbuluh. The cruel beating of Pastor seemed to last for hours and long after he had been carried into the barracks, Satiyah had stood beside the wall, her upper torso not moving but her legs shaking uncontrollably. When the morning train from Pakanbaru arrived she found herself still in place, unable to move.

Every time one of the Seraju Dal Spoorweg Maatschapij trains passed by their house, Satiyah would run outside calling "Papa! Papa!" Even as a student at the Angka Loro School, which was long before Ndoro Alimin began to teach there, whenever a train passed by she would try to peek out the window. If a train passed by the school during recess Satiyah would run to the middle of the school yard and begin to dance and shout. "Papa! Papa!" she still cried. All the other children envied her and if her father was on the train, he would stick out his hand and wave his arm with pride. "That's my daughter," he'd say to the stoker. "She's in school because I want a better life for her." He never did say a better life than whose.

Satiyah's father's hopes were realized when Ndoro Alimin proposed to her. The old man once remarked to his fellow workers: "It wasn't a waste of time for my daughter to go to school. Not a waste at all. Now she's going to be the wife of a teacher."

Was Ose a man accustomed to inflicting the cruelty she had witnessed? Perhaps he had been one of the men who tortured Ndoro Alimin, her husband. No, that wasn't possible. The two places were far distant. What's more, Ose was too kindhearted to have done anything like that. Shinji, that evil man. He could have. But supposing that he had been patient and treated her kindly as Masta had, she might have been willing to dedicate herself even to him. He was taller, fairer, and a more handsome and livelier man than Masta but she would never forgive him for that one

151

mistake. Even Misran had more feelings than he; at least he had not tried to hurt her.

By midday Satiyah's fear and her trembling had begun to subside. She was grateful that Ose had not been on the morning train but now it wouldn't be too long before the evening train arrived. Satiyah bathed and began to clean the house.

When the evening train arrived and Ose returned to his hut, tea was waiting for him on the table. Ose ignored the tea, unrolled his mat behind the screen, and lay down. He lay there for quite some time, not moving but not sleeping either. Satiyah was sure that he wasn't sleeping. Her heart began to race again.

The last train to pass through Taratakbuluh, the return train from Sijunjung to Pakanbaru, had come and gone some time before Ose suddenly rose from his mattress and went out to the back to bathe. After bathing, Ose sat at the table and poured tea for himself before Satiyah had a chance to help him.

"Are you still fasting, Satiyah-san?" he asked.

"Yes, Masta."

"What time do you eat?"

"Later, when the drum sounds."

"What time is that?"

"About eight thirty."

"Serve the food here and eat with me, will you?"

Satiyah found herself unable to reply.

"Will you?" Ose pressed.

"Yes, Masta. I will."

Satiyah was obviously nervous. She didn't know what she was supposed to feel.

❧

Lieutenant Ose left his hut and walked to the security post. The seven o'clock bell had rung. His men, in full dress and with their weapons, had been waiting for him for more than an hour and were now sitting around the yard in front of the security post. Upon sight of him they stood at once and moved into a line. Sergeant Kiguchi approached and saluted.

"Call the men into formation," Ose ordered.

"The Dutch too?"

"No. Later, alone."

The ten Dai Nippon soldiers spread out in pairs, one behind the other, facing east with their backs to the security post. Before them was the bamboo flagpole with the *Hinomaru* hanging limply from the top. The flag hardly moved. The camp was so protected it was almost impossible for the weak mid-dry-season wind to unfurl the flag. Ose stood on the makeshift podium near the flagpole.

After Sergeant Kiguchi presented his report, Ose took over the ceremony. The men were ordered at ease and then called back into formation. Ose turned his body swiftly toward the right to lead the ceremony of allegiance to *Tennō Heika*.

"*Sei-kerei!* Bow to the glory of *Tennō Heika!*"

My voice is too shrill, Ose thought as the men bowed their bodies at the waist as a sign of respect to *Tennō Heika*, their emperor in Tokyo.

"Heads up!"

He tempered the tone of his voice.

"In memory of the souls of fallen heroes, a moment of silence!"

The men bowed their heads.

"Heads up."

Each of the men began to wonder what was happening. Ose too seemed confused. What was he to say next? He had conducted this ceremony only as a means of finding the proper way to inform his men of the news he was obliged to convey.

"We shall now sing the *Kimigayo*," he said and then gave the proper pitch.

The *Kimigayo* is a slow song, possibly the slowest national anthem in the world, but the men's voices as they sang trembled with true emotion. That was the way they always sang it. This time they sang it twice. "At ease!" Ose ordered.

The soldiers relaxed. Some looked around with confusion on their faces.

"Men . . ." Ose began, then paused, "the war is over."

From the throats of a few of the men came a sound impossible to describe. All of the men stood nervously in place.

"Yesterday, at midday, Tokyo issued the order for the Dai Nippon Army to cease all forms of aggression but to continue to guard the stability and maintain the administration of the local government until such time as further orders are given."

Why am I lying? Ose asked himself. He could not make himself say that the Dai Nippon Army had surrendered and that *Tennō Heika* himself had delivered the announcement. At this moment here, in front of his men, he suddenly felt himself to be one of them, sharing their hopes and dreams.

Now, finally, he felt that he too was part of this war and part of the people involved in it. He was no longer a spectator but a participant who had helped to lead the ten men under him to shame and defeat.

Kiguchi raised his hand. Ose ignored him. He knew what the sergeant intended to ask and was desperately searching for a way to avoid giving an answer.

"Have we surrendered?" Kiguchi asked.

Ose gave Kiguchi no chance to question further. He proceeded with his speech as if no question had been asked.

"It is our responsibility to maintain the safety and the security of the people of this country. The trains will continue to run but other forms of labor will stop. All troops are to be withdrawn to Pakanbaru. This operation may begin at any time. We here in Taratakbuluh will, if possible, return to Pakanbaru tomorrow on the morning train. If not, we will return the following day, on the Saturday morning train. After you have been dismissed you are to return to

154

the barracks, pack your bags, and prepare for the soonest possible departure. Do not destroy the building. Leave everything as it is. Are there any questions?"

Ose had surprised even himself by being able to speak so fast and so clearly in such a situation.

The soldiers looked confused. That the war would end had long been the stuff for jokes among them. Now it had and they had been caught off guard. Many of the men were still in shock. Who among them hadn't heard Kiguchi's question? Lieutenant Ose had clearly avoided giving an answer. What else was there to ask? That was the most essential question, wasn't it? It appeared that Dai Nippon had surrendered. No one, however, wanted to cause the commander to lose face. Therefore, it was impossible to ask the question again.

"Are the Dutch to be taken to Pakanbaru too?" one of the men asked.

"Yes, the Dutch are to be taken to Pakanbaru."

"Will the coal train continue to run?"

"No, I suspect not."

"Is another team to be brought in to continue work on the embankment?"

"I don't know, but I think not."

Ose felt a great deal of respect for his men's behavior. They understood and therefore acted wisely. At the very least they were doing their utmost to avoid causing loss of face. At first they had seemed confused and nervous, shifting to the left and right, not seeming to know what to do with their hands. Now, awareness of the new facts of life appeared to be entering their subconscious. Their faces began to change and show a sense of calm and acceptance. The sense of self-worth, lost for a moment, was coming back, but it was a new sense of self-worth that showed on their faces—it was the self-worth of men who have been defeated.

These innocent men. What are they thinking about? Ose wondered. Are they suffering? Clearly they were disappointed but suffering was not readily apparent. People like

155

them, soldiers and other subordinates, seemed to be made of a stronger mettle. Suffering touched them but did not pierce their skin. Still, with their mouths slightly open and their chins jutting slightly forward, the men's faces looked unusually long and seemed to convey sadness and pity.

"If there are no more questions, we will lower the flag. Once you have been dismissed, bring the Dutch detainees here."

Ose himself led the flag-lowering ceremony, complete with singing of *Kimigayo* and *sei-kerei*. Then, on his orders, Sergeant Kiguchi stepped forward, turned right, and dismissed the men.

Three soldiers proceeded to the detainees' barracks to call the Dutch, but after arriving there suddenly came running back, crying out in surprise. Everyone turned. Sergeant Kiguchi ran up to them and immediately became engaged in a loud and hurried conversation. He then ran back to Ose who was already making his way toward the barracks. The sergeant saluted clumsily.

"The Dutch are not in their barracks," he reported, out of breath.

Lieutenant Ose tried to conceal his surprise. He walked in normal stride to the barracks, entered, and, with his eyes, surveyed the now-darkening room. He knew immediately what had happened and laughed nervously to himself but then felt sadness and guilt rise inside him. Supposing that he had conveyed the news immediately, the Dutch would still be here, undoubtedly singing and shouting with happiness while they, the Japanese, would be forced to watch. The indescribable mixture of emotions he could see pictured on the men's faces—the shame, sadness, disappointment, hurt, and pain—made him almost relieved the Dutch had escaped.

He looked at his subordinates one by one and saw disappointment and hope for forgiveness on their faces. They looked confused and at a complete loss as to what to do.

"Go after them, catch them, and bring them here. If necessary, shoot them."

At first the men didn't know how to respond, but when

the awareness that the order was serious finally began to sink in, the blood rose to their faces. They unclamped their bayonets, fixed them in position on the ends of their rifles, and took off, running toward the opening through which the Dutch had escaped.

❀

The Dutch ate much earlier than usual that day. The porridge that Freddie and Kliwon had made was still hot but they began to eat anyway. Some of the men sat inside the barracks. Others sat at the table outside. The tension in the air seemed to stifle any desire there might have been to talk. Freddie took a bowl of porridge to van Roscott.

"Eat, pastor," Wimpie told him.

The man addressed neither spoke nor moved in response.

After their meal the men took turns going down to the river to bathe and look at their fish traps. One by one they finished and returned to the barracks. There they waited. And waited more.

"They're lining up for roll call," one of the men said.

"They're in full uniform and have their weapons with them."

The men tried to see what was happening outside, all the while exchanging glances, trying to figure out what the ceremony meant. Kliwon didn't understand Dutch but pressed his eye to the wall too.

They heard the Japanese singing the *Kimigayo.*

"They're up to something. We should make our break now while there's still time," Wimpie advised.

"I think the war is over."

That was the voice of Pastor van Roscott. Rising slowly into sitting position, he looked at the other detainees. They turned back to look at him.

"Eat your meal, Pastor," Wimpie said. "After they've finished singing they're going to come here and shoot us all. Better to have a full stomach when you die because the road to heaven is a long one."

The impact of Wimpie's words was startling. The Dutch looked around in fear. Pastor felt only sadness. The men considered Wimpie's joke serious and his own seriousness, a joke. Perhaps the joke was the more logical answer. Given Japanese behavior and the serious tone of their voices, why not? He no longer had the strength to challenge this opinion. His desire to defend himself and his own opinions had completely vanished.

Slowly he lifted the bowl of porridge that Freddie had brought him earlier and along with the porridge he swallowed his tears and heartache.

Outside, Ose was speaking.

Bundles of provisions came out from beneath the *balai* and were piled in the corner closest to the spot at which Kliwon pointed. Kliwon slipped the covered *parang* that Lena had given him into his waistband.

It was light outside but beginning to grow dark in the room. Freddie hadn't bothered to build a fire and they weren't allowed to light torches without permission. The men looked around in the barracks' dusky light. Tension was building. Time stood still. Slowly and very carefully Wimpie and Kliwon began cutting a hole in the thatch wall. The men held their breaths as the hole opened up.

Wimpie jumped outside and was followed by Kliwon and a few of the rest. Their eyes searched for the stunted rubber tree that Paktua Hasan had mentioned to Kliwon. They found it and saw an open place in the brush beside it. The hole was only about two meters from the side of the barracks but they would have to crawl on their bellies to reach it. If they weren't careful, Lieutenant Ose who was facing west might catch sight of them.

The bundles were handed out. Now everyone was outside except for the Pastor. He sat silently on the *balai* looking around him sadly.

The men heard the *Kimigayo* once more.

"They're singing it again?"

"This it it!"

"Let's get out of here!"

"Now!"

Wimpie, Kliwon, then Freddie fell to their hands and knees and began to crawl toward the stunted tree. Arriving there, they jumped inside the opening and began running down the path toward freedom.

Pastor looked around again. It was so quiet. And now, growing dark. Thoughts tumbled through his mind. Could he sleep here alone? Could he face the wrath of the Japanese alone?

The last refrain of the *Kimigayo* faded. Pastor stopped thinking and jumped out of the barracks to plunge into the brush and follow the footsteps of his friends.

❀

After the initial shock of seeing Lena subsided, Paktua Hasan tried to convince her that what she was doing was very dangerous.

"But I must go with Kliwon," the girl insisted.

"I think it would be best if you both stayed here," Hasan advised. "I can take the Dutch by myself."

"If you can convince Kliwon not to go, that would be best." To herself, Lena wondered if that were true. Kliwon had been so insistent on going; there must be a reason.

Hours passed while the old man and the young woman waited. Lena sat on the river bank and Paktua Hasan squatted nearby.

"Why are you so stubborn about going alone?" Paktua Hasan finally asked Lena.

Lena's eyes opened wide. She stared at the man a long time before answering.

"Father wants to marry me off to one of those Minang traders."

"You could say no, couldn't you?"

Lena frowned. Why couldn't the old man understand her real reason for going?

"Last night Kliwon took my virginity," she finally answered.

Paktua Hasan said nothing.

They continued to wait, constantly having to defend themselves against the swarms of mosquitoes. It wasn't until *magrib* that they heard the sound of breaking twigs. A moment later Wimpie appeared, followed by Kliwon and the other detainees.

"Hey, he's got a woman along!" Wimpie screamed as soon as he saw Lena.

Kliwon ran toward Lena and the girl stood up to greet him.

"What are you doing here?" he asked her.

"I'm going with you," she said calmly.

"This is dangerous, Lena. Go home. I promise to come back."

"I'm going with you."

"No, you're not, Lena."

"Then you come back with me and face my father."

"Aw, let her come along, Kliwon. If you don't want her, you can give her to me," Wimpie said before bursting into laughter, the first laugh the men had heard since tasting freedom.

Wimpie's laughter rankled Kliwon but Lena burst out in anger. "You bastard!" she screamed at him.

Wimpie shrugged his shoulders and turned to Paktua Hasan. "Where to, old man?"

Paktua Hasan led the group to the crossing over the swamp. Wimpie stood at the beginning of the footbridge to keep the other men in single file behind Paktua Hasan. Kliwon and Lena stood stiffly in place, not saying a word.

Wimpie waited for the other men to cross. Then, just as he was about to step onto the bridge, he heard the sound of breaking branches. He first thought it was the Japanese but then it was van Roscott who appeared.

"I'm coming with you," he said in Dutch with a tone of hopelessness in his voice.

"What a coincidence this is," Wimpie remarked. "Now that we've got a pastor we might be able to arrange a marriage. We got a woman over there," Wimpie said in Indonesian.

Kliwon was growing increasingly anxious about going along. "Come on, Kliwon!" Wimpie shouted as he put his foot on the bridge. "If you don't, I'm going to tell everyone your secret."

Kliwon said nothing. Pastor looked at the two men and knew immediately what each was thinking. He approached Kliwon and Lena and stood in front of them.

160

"You should not be going with us," he told them.

Wimpie had already proceeded to the third trunk, the middle section of the rickety footbridge. There he took the rope that he had brought along and tied one end around the base of the trunk on which he was standing. Holding the other end of the rope in his hand, he continued across the swamp.

"What are you doing?" Paktua Hasan shouted at Wimpie.

Wimpie paid no attention to the man.

"Hey, Pastor, Kliwon, bring that woman here! On the double! The Japs are going to be here soon," he shouted in Indonesian.

Wimpie was right. No sooner had he said that when out from the brush came the Japanese soldiers, the bared bayonets on their rifles still visible in the fading light. Wimpie pulled the rope in his hands.

"Don't! Don't!" Paktua Hasan shouted, hoping to stop him.

Freddie grabbed the old man and held him tightly.

The footbridge collapsed and the tree trunks crashing through the brush, the reeds, and the water below raised a roar, a splash, and a host of quail. The birds raced skyward with the beating of their wings adding to the commotion below.

Wimpie pulled a small blade from his waist and placed its point at Paktua Hasan's throat.

"Get us out of here!" he ordered.

Paktua Hasan said nothing. He looked calmly into Wimpie's eyes, then turned and began to walk, followed by Wimpie and the other detainees.

❖

Shortly before *magrib*, Haji Usman, Anis, and Sutan Mudo arrived at Haji Zen's house where they found their host sitting in the middle room. He looked nervous.

"Please, sit down. Join me," Haji Zen said to his guests after first returning their initial greetings.

"I'm afraid I don't know where Lena is," he said immediately.

The men sat down.

At that same moment Haji Deramah came running into the house looking confused and completely out of breath.

"She's not there," she said excitedly to her husband. "She's not at Jamilah's house and isn't at any of her other friends' either. No one has seen her all day."

Haji Zen stared. His guests said nothing.

"She must have run off with Kliwon," he finally said, hoping the shock he felt did not show.

"*Astagafirullah!* May God forgive me!" Haji Deramah screamed. "How could she have run away? Who is to blame for this!" she cried at her husband.

"We'll go after them," Haji Zen said to his wife.

"But where?" his wife screamed.

"I know. Follow me!" Haji Zen then said to his three guests: "When it's time to break fast, please go ahead. Don't wait for me."

Haji Zen and his wife ran out of the house and off in the direction of the railroad trestle.

Haji Usman didn't know what to do.

"Stay here," he told Anis and Sutan Mudo. "Go ahead and break fast if you want."

The two Minang traders nodded.

Haji Usman ran out of the house, following Haji Zen and Haji Deramah across the trestle.

❁

The Japanese soldiers didn't know what to do. The bridge over the swamp had collapsed. Ose, who had followed his men through the brush, made a quick survey of the scene and knew what had happened. He felt disappointed.

Kiguchi and the other soldiers surrounded the three people who had been left behind: Pastor, Kliwon, and Lena. None of the soldiers had ever seen Lena but even in the fading light they could tell that she was beautiful. She held herself well, straight and upright in an almost masculine manner. Taller than average, her skin was smooth and copper-colored and her large, round eyes, finely bridged nose and full lips made her a pleasure to see. A few strands

162

of hair had fallen across her forehead but behind her two thick black braids hung down past her waist.

Kliwon looked pale and afraid but was trying to smile. With his stooped shoulders and torso bent slightly forward he appeared to be trying to make his body as small as possible. The covered *parang* that Lena had given him was not in his waistband. It had fallen to the ground earlier. It was a pity, Ose thought, for a girl of such fine appearance to have chosen a man like this.

Pastor didn't smile but showed no fear either; anger and bitterness were in his eyes. He made no attempt to pray. Instead, he looked around at the Japanese, staring at them one by one. His head stopped at Kiguchi and the unfathomable hatred apparent in his eyes caused the Japanese sergeant to tremble and fall back slightly.

Ose saw all of this clearly. The quail had returned to their nests and silence blanketed the scene. The wind barely moved. Faintly, from the direction they had come, came the sound of the drum for *magrib* prayers.

The three people had no idea what kind of fate awaited them.

"Shoot!" Ose cried out.

Ten guns spat bullets and flames. Thunder rolled and the three fell without even a chance to scream. The soldiers fired again and again until all their bullets had been spent. Sergeant Kiguchi jumped forward and plunged his bayonet into Pastor's body, now little more than a pile of meat wrapped in a bloody and soiled cloth.

The quail rose in flight once more with their wings beating a low and swift path.

Haji Zen, Haji Deramah, and Haji Usman found the barracks completely empty. They were just entering the brush near the stunted rubber tree when they heard the sound of repeated gunshots.

"Lena!" Haji Deramah screamed repeatedly. "My baby, my Lena."

The two men said nothing. Half running, half walking, they traced the path that the detainees and the Japanese soldiers had followed earlier.

Satiyah lighted palm oil lamps and candles and placed them around the middle room and the low table in its center. Food waited on the table; a small bowl of *kolak*, the sweetened stew for breaking fast, was there too. Outside, it was silent. She sensed that something was wrong and all of a sudden felt completely alone in a strange and foreign world. The Dutch and the Japanese had suddenly vanished and now she was alone, completely alone. She peeked outside through the cracks in the wall but could see nothing. She allowed herself to feel neither hope nor worry.

Hearing voices, Satiyah peeked outside again, this time to see three old people running into the barracks of the Dutch. The woman was screaming hysterically.

She heard the sound of the drum.

And ate her sweetened stew.

With the sound of repeated gunshots.

She served herself rice and began to eat.

❄

The clock on the security post table showed almost eleven o'clock, Tokyo time. Pastor had been buried without ceremony at the site where he was killed and now people from the village were walking by the post with the other two corpses. They had wanted to leave Kliwon's body behind but Haji Zen had insisted that it be carried back. Lieutenant Ose had agreed. The group was a large one, about fifty people in all, each with a torch in his hand.

The procession moved slowly and from a distance all that was visible was the light of the torches, a floating stream of flame, a swarm of fireflies that appeared then disappeared behind the trees. Now going up the embankment, now moving slowly across the trestle, and now descending on the other side in the direction of Haji Zen's home. It was a scene that conveyed an impression of devotion, holiness, and calm. Few people in the group spoke; those who did, spoke in whispers.

Ose drew in a deep sigh of relief and stood.

"There is no need for guard duty tonight. No bells need be rung. Tonight everyone shall sleep."

164

The soldiers barely heard what Ose had said. They were swept away in their own thoughts about what had happened. Ose allowed them to continue thinking undisturbed while he walked quickly toward his hut. Satiyah was waiting for him.

"I ate already, Masta," she told him.

Ose said nothing and sat down, trying not to reveal his emotions.

"Would you like to eat, Masta?"

"Yes."

Satiyah served Ose his food and after he had finished eating, cleared the table. Ose remained seated, watching Satiyah as she finished her work and retreated into her doorless room.

For some time Ose said nothing but then called softly, "Satiyah-san."

Satiyah came out of her room and approached him.

"Sit down," Ose said to her.

Satiyah did as she was told but kept her eyes fixed on him. What is it? she wondered as her thoughts roamed between hope and anxiousness.

"What village do you come from?" Ose asked.

What an odd question, Satiyah thought. What was Masta really asking?

"From Mersi, Masta, in Java, near Purwokerto," she answered hesitantly.

"Is your family there?"

"My children are and my mother and father. My younger brothers and sisters too."

"How many children do you have?"

"Three, Masta . . . two now. One died."

"Where is your husband?"

"He's dead too, Masta."

How very little he really knows about me, Satiyah thought. But then, she asked herself, what did she know about him? She suddenly realized how foreign they really were to each other but, just as suddenly, knew that she loved this foreign man.

"Satiyah-san . . . do you want to go home?"

165

Satiyah grew more confused. Her hesitation increased. "No, Masta. I am happy here."

Ose stared in silence at the face of the pretty woman in front of him and in doing so, came to know what he too felt.

"Life is difficult there, Masta," Satiyah added, half lying.

Ose stood and walked to the corner of the room where his trunk of clothing sat. He took a key, opened the lock, and from the trunk withdrew the bundle with the dirty cloth wrap that Shinji had given him in Singapore. After sitting down at the table once more, he placed the bundle on top of the table and opened it.

Satiyah's eyes blinked at the sight of so much jewelry. She had never dreamed that Masta was storing such an incredible cache of gold and diamonds in this place. She thought immediately of Surti, the village girl who had become the mistress of the *ndoro tuan* from the city. But even her jewelry, the jewelry she had worn on that historic night, was of no comparison to what was lying on the table before her in an old dirty cloth.

"Go home, Satiyah," Ose said, "this is for you. Take them all. Sell them as you need to so that you can live happily. Buy a rice field, land, cows, goats."

Satiyah lowered her head, her heart pounding in her chest and her blood rushing to her face. Then, thinking of Ose, her "masta," a sense of fear and worry took her and she lifted her eyes from the jewelry to Ose's face.

"What about you, Masta?" she asked him.

The man's face moved with unspoken emotion. His lips, then his voice trembled as he spoke. "Satiyah-san," he said weakly, "Nippon has lost."

The news came as a shock. Satiyah's mouth dropped open and her eyes blinked in disbelief at the truth on Ose's face. She shook her head back and forth.

"It's true, Satiyah-san. Nippon is defeated," Ose repeated again.

"No, no . . ." Satiyah said as she shook her head.

"Yes, Satiyah. Nippon is lost. Soon the Americans will come and all the Japanese will be taken away."

"No!" the woman screamed.

Satiyah's scream was so loud that even she herself was surprised. Ose placed his index finger on her lips.

Silence returned. Outside, it was quiet too. The soldiers were fast asleep.

"It will be hard for me, Satiyah-san. It doesn't have to be hard for you. You are a good person, Satiyah-san. It will be all right for you."

Tears began to well up in Satiyah's eyes. Alimin, she thought, why have you cursed me so? She continued staring at Ose.

"The Americans will come and I will be captured. You go home to your village, Satiyah-san."

Satiyah bit her lips to hold back her tears but then began to sob.

"Come with me, Masta. We can run away and stay here in the village. Then we can go back to my village. We can live there."

"I can not run away, Satiyah-san," Ose said soothingly.

"If you can't run, then I will go with you, Masta."

Satiyah moved toward Ose, bringing her body close to his. Ose too could no longer restrain his tears. He began to sob and stroke Satiyah's hair.

"Don't come with me, Satiyah-san. Go home to your village. Be a good person. Take care of your children. Don't follow me."

Satiyah wept without control. She took the hand that was now stroking her hair and placed it on her mouth. She kissed its fingers, then pressed it to her breast. Ose made no attempt to stop her. Their eyes met. They cried, their bodies heaved with their sobs; they looked at each other, and they cried.

Ose threw his other arm around Satiyah and began to kiss her cheeks, her eyes, her forehead, her chin, her lips. Satiyah pressed her lips to his, giving him her cries and tears. Slowly, gradually, their kisses softened and a smoldering warmth began to enclose them. Their breathing came in starts.

"Masta," Satiyah whispered, "sleep with me."

Glossary

adat. customs, tradition.

alun-alun. a city square or park used for playground, sport, military drill parades, and mass meetings.

anak-pisang. literally, the offshoots of a banana tree; however, the term also refers to the children born from the union of a Minangkabau man and a non-Minangkabau woman.

asar. for Moslems, the afternoon prayer at 4 P.M. or, as a time marker, the period between 3 P.M. and 5 P.M.

assalam'alaikum. "Peace be unto you," a greeting commonly used among Moslems.

asso-ka. "Really?" or "Is that so?" (Japanese).

astaga. "May God forgive me" (Arabic).

babelok. a Minangkabau term for traveling salesmen.

balai. a low bed or a sitting or sleeping area usually made from bamboo.

banzai. a cheer or battle cry; literally, "victory."

bapak. literally, father, but also a term of address used when speaking to older, usually married, males.

Batavia. the name for Jakarta when Indonesia was under the Dutch.

belati. a small daggerlike knife.

blangkon. male Javanese batik headdress.

Bu. colloquial for *Ibu.*

Bulan Puasa. literally, fasting month, which for Indonesian Moslems is the same as Ramadan.

Dai Nippon. Japan, or Great Japan.

gamelan. Javanese orchestra.

God verdomme. "God damn it!" (Dutch).

gotong royong. the Indonesian concept of working together; mutual cooperation.

Greater East Asia Co-Prosperity Sphere. the region including Korea, Manchuria, China, French Indochina, Malaya, Burma, the Philippines, and the East Indies, as well as the Japanese empire as it existed prior to the Manchurian Incident, which the Japanese, during World War II, hoped to unite under its authority.

hai. Japanese interjection often meaning "yes" or "I understand."

haji. one who has made the pilgrimage to Mecca; in Indonesia a term of address (for males and females alike).

hara-kiri. a vulgar term for self-disembowelment (*seppuku*).

heitei. soldier.

High Malay. formal Malay language, as opposed to "low" or "market Malay."

Hinomaru. The Rising Sun—the Japanese national flag.

hiragana. one of the two syllabaries of modern Japanese (the other being *katagana*). Hiragana, developed from the "grass hand" (shorthand) form of characters, are the squarish symbols used as a kind of italics to write foreign words or unusual terms.

hutan. jungle or forest.

ibu. literally, mother, but, in Indonesia, used as a term of address for older or married women.

imam. Moslem religious leader.

isa. evening prayer or time period (approximately 8 P.M.).

jibaku. Japanese for a war of no surrender or self-destruction.

jujitsu. Japanese art of weaponless fighting employing holds, throws, and paralyzing blows to disable an opponent.

kadhi. Moslem judge.

kain. wraparound cloth, usually of batik, worn by Indonesian women.

kak. short form of *kakak,* meaning older brother or sister.

kakak. older brother or sister; also a term of address for older friends.

kami. in the Shinto system of beliefs, the forces of nature. Often translated as 'gods' or 'deities,' *kami,* in fact, means 'above,' 'superior,' or 'divine,' and signifies anything that is an object of reverence and respect.

kangmas. older brother, but also a term of address for a husband or sweetheart.

katagana. one of the two syllabaries of modern Japanese.

kebaya. a type of blouse that reaches below the waist and is often made of light material with embroidered edges.

kelurahan. village or ward administrative unit (see *lurah*).

ketupat. rice cooked in a small container made of plaited coconut leaves, most often served during the holidays that follow Ramadan.

khatib. a mosque official or anyone, religious or lay, who delivers the Islamic sermon.

Kimigayo. the Japanese national anthem.

kolak. fruit stewed with brown palm sugar.

konban-wa. "Good evening" (Japanese).

kongsi. originally a Chinese term that, in Indonesian, means a commercial partnership or association.

Kota. old section of Jakarta.

kyai. Islamic teacher, scholar, or leader; also a term of address.

langgar. village mosque or prayer house.

Lebaran. day ending the fasting period.

lohor. prayer or time period from 11:50 A.M. to 2:30 P.M.

lurah. village chief (see *kelurahan*).

magrib. sunset or sunset prayer.

mas. sir, brother (used to address older contemporaries, including wife to husband).

masta. from the English "master"; this term of address was used by Indonesian civilians when speaking with Japanese (males) during the Japanese occupation.

Menteng. elite, formerly Dutch, section of Jakarta.

merantau. the verb form of the root word *rantau*, meaning to leave one's home area (especially that of the Minangkabaus).

Minang. short form of Minangkabau, the people that inhabit the western part of Sumatra.

MULO. the abbreviation for Meer Uitgebreid Lagere Onderwijs, a junior high school started by the Dutch in Indonesia for Dutch and native children from grades 8 through 10.

ndoro. Javanese term of address used when speaking with older males of a higher station.

ndoro tuan. Javanese-Indonesian term of address used when speaking with older foreign (Dutch) males.

ohayo, gozaimas. "Good morning" (Japanese).

pak. short form of *bapak*, meaning father or sir.

paktua. from *Bapak Tua*, or older father, a term of address for elderly males.

pandan. plant whose leaves are used for making mats, hats, and other woven articles.

parang. short sword or knife.

pawang. guide with magical powers.

perahu. a kind of small boat.

perantau. a person, especially a Minangkabau, who travels away from home to seek his fortune (see *merantau*).

Petromax. brand name for a kind of pressurized kerosene lamp similar to a Coleman lantern.

pici. type of cap, usually of black velvet.

ploeg. from Dutch, a whistle stop or security post along the railroad line.

pomat. the second call to prayer.

Ramadan. ninth month of the Arabic calendar (following Sya'-ban), the month for fasting.

ranah. Minangkabau word for ravine or valley.

romaji. Japanese written in the Latin alphabet.

romusha. in Indonesia, an involuntary worker for the Japanese during World War II.

sahur. postmidnight meal before daytime fasting during the fasting month.

sambal. hot sauce usually made from chilies.

-san. Japanese honorific.

santri. in Java, a person who is consciously and exclusively Moslem.

sarong. a wraparound cloth with its ends sewn together. In Indonesia, more often worn by males than females.

sei-kerei. a bow from the waist.

selamatan. religious or celebratory meal.

seppuku. ritual self-disembowelment.

sholat. from Arabic, to pray or to perform the five obligatory daily prayers.

Shonanto. literally, Southwest Island, the Japanese name for Singapore.

Showa. Divine Peace (Japanese), the name chosen by Hirohito for his reign.

silat. from *pencak-silat*, the Indonesian art of self-defense.

so-deska. short for *ah-so-deska*, meaning "Really?" or "Is that so?".

subhanahu wa ta'ala. "Praise be to God the Most Powerful" (Arabic).

subuh. dawn or early morning prayers.

sukoshi. a little (Japanese).

sumo. Japanese form of wrestling in which a contestant loses if he is forced out of the ring or if any part of his body except the soles of his feet touches the ground.

surau. religious training center for advanced Islamic students.

sutan. title of nobility in Sumatra.

sutan mudo. title of lesser nobility in Sumatra.

Sya'ban. eighth month of the Arabic calender.

syirik. to commit or be guilty of polytheism.

tadarusan. recitation of the Quran in rotation.

taiso. gymnastics or exercise.

tarawih. special evening prayers during the fasting month.
Tennō Heika. the Japanese emperor; literally, from Heaven.
tuan. "sir" or "Mr.," a term of address often used for foreign men.
wa'alaikum salam. "And peace be unto you," the common response to the greeting *"assalamu'alaikum."*
warung. small roadside stall or eating place.
wayang kulit. Javanese shadow-puppet theater.